USA TODAY BESTSELLING AUTHOR

NANCY WARREN

BLOOD, SWEAT AND TIERS

THE GREAT WITCHES BAKING SHOW
BOOK 5

Blood, Sweat and Tiers: The Great Witches Baking Show book 5

Copyright © 2021 by Nancy Warren

ISBN: ebook 978-1-928145-90-5

ISBN: print 978-1-928145-89-9

Cover Design by Lou Harper of Cover Affairs

Ambleside Publishing

INTRODUCTION

"I love cozy mysteries and The Great British Baking Show and this wonderfully quirky series combines them to perfection!"

The Earl of Frome gets a shock when a gaggle of nosy bird watchers gang up on him. When one of them winds up dead, it doesn't look good for the Earl. Amateur baker Poppy Wilkinson gets embroiled in yet another murder mystery. It's a good thing she's got witchy powers as she has to solve a murder, try and learn more about her own mysterious beginnings and turn out a winning cake, because it's cake week in the competition tent.

From USA Today Bestselling author Nancy Warren comes the 5th book in the witches baking series. Each book can be read alone. They feature no sex, gore or bad language but lots of clues, some quirky humor, and recipes. "Just my cup of tea--with cake!"

If you haven't met Rafe Crosyer yet, he's the gorgeous, sexy vampire in *The Vampire Knitting Club* series. You can get his origin story free when you join Nancy's no-spam newsletter at NancyWarrenAuthor.com.

Come join Nancy in her private Facebook group where we talk about books, knitting, pets and life.
www.facebook.com/groups/NancyWarrenKnitwits

BLOOD, SWEAT AND TIERS

CHAPTER 1

"Why is Lord Frome coming toward us with a rifle?" Florence whispered, moving so she stood behind Hamish's broad back. I looked up from my workstation in the competition tent on the grounds of Broomewode Hall in Somerset in the UK. It was Friday afternoon, and the three of us over-keen bakers had arrived early to prepare for this weekend's filming of *The Great British Baking Contest.* That is, if we could survive whatever the Earl of Frome was about to do with his rifle.

I'd never seen the Lord of the Manor inside the tent's crisp white awning before. Although he walked with long, purposeful strides, he looked awkward, totally out of sync with the bustling energy of the tent. It might have had something to do with his getup. I'd lived in the English countryside long enough to recognize that he and the man he was with were wearing hunting tweeds: wool caps, tweed jackets with matching vests over jodhpurs tucked into leather boots. Under the vest and jacket, they wore checked shirts with ties.

The whole thing was so elaborate, so traditional, it was almost farcical.

I looked back at Florence, who—ever the actor—was still playfully hiding behind Hamish, and laughed. "Don't worry," I told her. "He won't shoot us. He needs the money from *The Great British Baking Contest* to run the estate."

There was a muffled snicker from one of the technicians setting up the lights. Oops. I'd have to keep my voice down if I didn't want to start accidentally spreading local gossip.

Apart from the contestants, the tent was buzzing with staff from the show, checking sound and running through camera positions to make sure everything would be ready to roll for filming early tomorrow morning.

Hamish took a step away from Florence. "There's nothing to fear—that's a shotgun meant for hunting game, not killing people. Besides, it's broken, which means he can't shoot it."

Hamish was a police officer up in the Scottish Highlands, but he raised Shetland ponies and knew all about farming. By broken, I assumed he meant the way the barrel was bent away from the stock of the gun so it looked like a triangle.

Florence tucked a stray strand of chestnut hair behind her ears. She was wearing it in a high ponytail today and looked more casual than usual but still glamorous. But then the woman could have worn a flour sack with holes cut out for arms and look gorgeous.

The earl was crossing the tent now, with the second man following behind, also carrying a shotgun. To my horror, he was heading straight for us, but I couldn't imagine why. Was this another ploy to be *at one with the village people*? I grimaced as I remembered his and Lady Frome's little performance in the pub a couple of weeks ago, talking to the staff and customers as if they were one big happy family. No one had been fooled.

The earl stopped at Hamish's workstation. His shotgun tapped the floor as he let it rest by his side. "Good afternoon, bakers," he said in his posh voice. "How are you all getting on?"

"Fine, fine," Hamish said, and Florence and I nodded.

"Good, good," the earl echoed. He looked around the tent with an appraising eye, as if he were considering buying the place—pretty silly, considering the grounds belonged to his family.

There was a moment of silence, which not even the vivacious Florence attempted to break. I took the opportunity to study the earl's face. Just like the first time I met Lord Frome, I was struck by how much he looked like a cardboard cutout of an aristocrat. He must have been well into his fifties, but had a full head of neatly coiffed hair, gray now, but with a few lingering streaks of ashy brown. His deep brown eyes were close-set beside a strong, slightly pointed nose, which his son Benedict had inherited. The earl's pronounced chin was responsible for his overall haughty appearance, although the smile lines around his firmly set mouth went some way to softening the effect. I imagined he must have been quite formidable as a young man.

Fiona, the director, glanced at the rifle with horror. "Good afternoon, sir," she said, her eyes wandering back to the rifle. "Are you going shooting, sir?"

Could Fiona fit another *sir* in her short address? It was kind of troubling to see her so deferential when it was Fiona's orders we were used to following during a tough weekend's filming.

Lord Frome nodded. "Not to worry. Won't make a noise while you're filming. Thought I'd pop in and give you all my best. High time I saw what you all get up to in here." He made a grand, sweeping gesture before spying the bowl of fresh raspberries on Florence's workstation and smiling. "What lovely, fresh berries. Local, I imagine."

Florence, who had remained uncannily silent so far, suddenly appeared to remember that she was never one to pass up an opportunity for attention and flashed her most Oscar-acceptance-worthy smile. "Yes, Your Lordship. Please, help yourself."

He popped a red berry into his mouth and made noises indicative of pleasure. Florence said, "It's cake week, you see, Your Lordship. The judges want us to use some of the local fresh fruits. I've quite the penchant for juicy raspberries myself. These ones are especially sweet and tangy."

"Marvelous. Marvelous." Lord Frome nodded in agreement and then looked as though he hadn't the slightest clue what to say next. "Well, carry on, carry on. I shan't keep you from your work. I look forward to seeing your cakes."

And then he was gone.

The moment the earl was out of earshot, Hamish turned to Florence with a grin. "Your Lordship?"

"I looked up how one should address an earl for just such an occasion," she said with dignity.

We watched as Lord Frome and the man, who was presumably his gamekeeper, headed off down a path. The earl stumbled over a root and Hamish said, "Let's hope he doesn't shoot his own foot off."

"I doubt the earl is accident-prone," Florence said with a sniff. "He's far too composed."

I shrugged and went back to putting my ingredients away. The technicians continued to work around us, and Fiona and Donald, the series producer, went back to their meeting, no doubt discussing how our baking highs and lows would best be captured over the course of the weekend. For now, however, everything in the tent was calm. The calm before the storm.

But the peace didn't last long: I jumped when an almighty *CRAAAAACK CRACK CRACK* sounded in the distance.

"Was that gunfire?" Florence asked, half alarmed, half thrilled.

"Yup," Hamish said.

Fiona threw up her hands and addressed Donald with a look of despair. "So glad the good earl isn't going to make any noise," she said, her voice laced with sarcasm. She shook her head. "He knows full well that one of the most difficult things about filming outside is the extraneous noise. It makes everything so much harder."

Just then, the almighty roar of a lawn mower joined the chorus of gunshots.

"Oh, I give up," Donald muttered.

Fiona walked towards the entrance of the tent where Edward, the gardener, was mowing the vast green lawns that surrounded Broomewode Hall. She flapped her hands about to get his attention and, with a judder, Edward halted his mowing.

Before Fiona even opened her mouth, Edward assured her that all mowing duties would be finished before filming started tomorrow morning. She let out her breath in relief, and he gave her a cheeky smile.

"Wish I could guarantee the same for the boss man," he

continued, "but the earl raises grouse, quail, and pheasants, and he and his gamekeeper are after the vermin who eat the young chicks."

"Oh." Fiona looked crestfallen. "I'd assumed he was clay-pigeon shooting. Not killing live animals. I'm a vegetarian."

I was shocked. Like Fiona, I'd thought the earl was just killing time with sport, not creatures. I turned back to Florence and Hamish and chastised the two men for hunting.

"Brutal, isn't it?" Florence said, shaking her head so that her pretty curls tumbled over her forehead. "Who's to say what animals are vermin?"

"It's easy to think that way," Hamish said, "but it's legal to shoot magpies, crows, foxes, rats—any animals that hunt the baby quail and pheasant. As a bit of a farmer myself, I can tell you that landowners who raise game birds are also protecting the habitat for other birds. It's the natural cycle of things, pet," he added gently. "Mother Nature has her ways, and sometimes we give her a helping hand, that's all."

"I never knew old Hamish was such a poetic soul," said a voice from behind me.

I turned and there was Gerry, his ghostly form floating by the fridges and grinning away. Oh, great. I wanted to motion for him to vamoose—how many times did I have to remind him not to talk to me in front of people?—but how could I do that without the others noticing? Pretend to be swatting at a fly? Actually, come to think of it, Gerry's presence in the tent was a little like an annoying fly, buzzing in my ear.

As if he'd just read my thoughts, Gerry frowned and let out a big sigh. But luckily he hadn't managed to master mind-reading this week. "It's him again," Gerry said, pointing at the entrance to the tent. "Thinks he's God's gift. You should see

the way he struts around this place. Not my cup of tea at all."
I looked over and saw a new security guard talking to Donald.
Hamish and Florence followed my gaze.

"Who's that hot dish?" Florence asked, raising an eyebrow.

"Martin," Gerry replied.

"I've heard he's called Martin," I dutifully relayed. "He's new."

"How are you always so up to date with the goss round here?" Florence asked.

I imagined replying: *Well, the ghosts round here don't have a lot to do.*

I shrugged. Martin looked to be in his late thirties with a head of dark hair sharply parted to the side. He was wearing the gray security guard's uniform: smart trousers with a crease down the middle, walkie-talkie at the hip, and a short-sleeved shirt with the Broomewode crest. He was setting up the rope barrier by the tent, behind which some of the public were allowed to quietly watch us racing around the tent in a panic, brandishing our whisks like magic wands.

I couldn't believe filming was starting again already. I'd been floating all week after being crowned best baker last Sunday. But now that I was back in Broomewode, I'd come down to earth with a bump. The reality was you were only as good as your last bake. And after Priscilla's exit last week, the competition was toughening up. I had to prove myself worthy of staying on the show.

"I might just introduce myself to our newbie crew member," Florence said and sashayed off to flutter her eyelashes at the unsuspecting Martin. It was as much of a guess as to who Florence would date around here as it was who'd win the show. Darius, the Greek god who worked at the inn, had caught her attention last I'd seen.

"What do you have planned for your signature bake?" I asked Hamish, watching him unpack a whopping amount of oranges and lemons.

"It's a cake-inspired version of a St. Clements," Hamish said, looking at me as if I knew what he was talking about.

"St. Clements?" I asked.

There was a silence and then Hamish burst into song, his deep baritone echoing around the tent.

> *Oranges and lemons,*
> *Say the bells of St Clements.*
>
> *You owe me five farthings,*
> *Say the bells of St. Martins.*
>
> *When will you pay me?*
> *Say the bells at Old Bailey.*
>
> *When I grow rich,*
> *Say the bells at Shoreditch.*
>
> *When will that be?*
> *Say the bells of Stepney.*
>
> *I do not know,*
> *Says the great bell at Bow.*
>
> *Here comes a candle to light you to bed,*
> *And here comes a chopper to chop off your head!*

Chip chop chip chop the last man is dead!

My jaw dropped open.

"You've never heard that before? Sometimes I forget you grew up on the other side of the pond."

I shook my head. "What kind of sick nursery rhyme is that?"

Hamish chuckled. "So many childhood rhymes are terrifying. 'London Bridge Is Falling Down,' 'Pop Goes the Weasel,' and 'Ring a Ring of Roses,'" he said, ticking them off on his fingers. "All plague and misery. 'Oranges and Lemons' is based on a nursery rhyme which dates all the way to the eighteenth century. It name-checks all the major churches in London, starting with St. Clements because it has such an unusual peal of church bells. The oranges and lemons of the song refer to the cargo that would have been offloaded close to the church when the Thames was a lot farther in than it is today. My grandpa was born in central London, and he had a fruit stall in the East End, so the rhyme resonates with me. Good talking point for the show, right?"

I nodded. I bet he'd done some research, too. But I couldn't get over the last line and asked Hamish about the chopping of the head.

"Ach, yes, there's lots of speculation about those lines, but what *I* think makes most sense is that it's referring to Newgate prison—next to the Old Bailey church in the rhyme. The church had a great tenor bell, and at nine a.m. on Monday mornings, it would ring out to signal the start of any hangings due to take place that week. The prisoners on death row were visited the night before by the bell man of St. Sepulchre, who would hold a candle in one hand and ring the execution bell in the other."

I shuddered. "That is one seriously messed-up nursery rhyme to sing to kids."

"I agree, but the oranges and lemons make for a tasty cake." Hamish tossed an orange in the air and caught it, and went on to explain that he was making a light sponge sandwiched with orange curd, cloaked in lemon icing and finished with a lemon syrup drizzle. He was still undecided about the decorations (a relief, as I was, too) but he'd been playing around with various arrangements of sliced candied oranges and lemons.

As he spoke, I set about putting my dry ingredients away —I was due over at Susan Bentley's farm soon to pick up some fresh produce. I was going to make a four-tier strawberry and basil layer cake. It was my riskiest ingredient combo to date, and I'd had a tough week getting the balance of this one right.

"Should we save poor Martin from Florence?" Hamish asked, gesturing at where our friend had backed the security guard into a corner of the tent. Even from here, I could see that he was perspiring at the temples. Florence tended to have this effect on men. She was so gorgeous and so confident that the men she flirted with turned to wobbling jelly the moment she switched on her charms. The new barman at the inn, Darius, was the only man I'd seen hold his own around Florence. My bets were on him.

Under the guise of getting some lunch, I took Florence by the arm and led her out of the tent. Hamish followed. It was a gorgeous day, and I lifted my face skyward to feel the sun's soft embrace. The manicured lawns were bathed in a golden glow, and I stepped out onto the thick, springy green grass. I closed my eyes for a moment and reminded myself how lucky I was to have gotten this far in the competition. The scent of magnolias carried on the breeze, and I opened my eyes to see a pretty bed bursting with their white and pink star-shaped blooms.

"Every weekend we get to be back here feels like a dream," Hamish said, following my gaze.

I nodded solemnly. A dream I didn't want to wake from.

Florence took my arm, and when we'd gotten far enough to be out of earshot, she told us what "a dish" Martin was. "He used to be in the navy," she said. "Imagine his levels of fitness. Why, I bet he could bench-press three hundred pounds."

I laughed. Florence's enthusiasm was infectious. Not that I thought Martin was "a dish," as she put it, but I liked how she always found something to compliment people about.

But the peace was shattered by more gunshots echoing through the air. Florence almost jumped out of her skin, although I suspected that most of that was practice for the stage. Or the cameras, which I couldn't forget would be trained on us for the next forty-eight hours. I gulped.

I turned to look in the direction of where the awful sound still crackled in the air and spotted a beautiful bird of prey swoop through the air. I stopped in my tracks and raised a hand to my eyes, shielding against the glare of the sun, and let Hamish and Florence walk on. I squinted. Was that a hawk? The bird came closer, as if he could feel my eyes on him. Maybe I was acting crazy, but I could have sworn that it was the same hawk I'd seen in the tree by the Orangery last week. He was so majestic, and as he soared by my head, I caught sight of his plumage, the scattering of white on his rich brown body, the cinnamon-red of his tail. His beak was curved and sharp.

Was this a good portent? I couldn't be sure, but one thing I did know was that I was going to have to bake my witchy socks off this week. And if a sighting of a hawk might rouse the same kind of luck as my winning bake last week, well then, bring it on. I murmured a silent thank-you to the bird, wishing him well like I did my cakes as they went into the oven. I jogged to catch up with Hamish and Florence, who'd wandered on, oblivious to my moment with the hawk—which was probably for the best. What with ghosts and my familiar, Gateau, I had my work cut out for me not looking like I was talking to thin air.

CHAPTER 2

"*L*unch, I think," Florence said and Hamish agreed. As much as I'd have loved to languish all afternoon in the pub with those two, I had to get over to Susan Bentley's farm. She'd messaged me Wednesday to say a small crop of strawberries in her back garden had come up trumps and would I be interested, which was music to my ears, of course. I was hoping she'd also have a few eggs from her happy hens to give my cake an extra helping hand. I told them to save me some food, and that I'd catch up with them later.

I collected Gateau, who'd been napping in my room and was less than impressed at me rousing her from her kitten dreams, and we headed down the now familiar path to the farm.

She trotted along by my side, every so often stopping to rub her little nose against the blooms spilling out from the flowerbeds on either side of the path. Each week I returned to Broomewode Village, it felt like a new type of flower had blossomed. Now that it was June, bright blue geraniums and beetroot-blotched oriental poppies had joined the beds of pink azaleas and yellow freesias. The multi-colored pansies I'd admired a couple of weeks ago were wilting a little now, but more puffy heads of alliums had sprung up around them. The crowd of foxgloves had grown, and their tender, lovely stems aroused mixed feelings in me. I remembered poor Eileen and her troublesome heart, how foxgloves could be used to both help and hinder angina. But I also recalled how my flower sketches for the garden magazine had been so well received. As a freelance graphic designer and illustrator, I hoped to have more jobs like that when my time in the competition came to an end.

But as soon as I had the thought, I realized it was hard to imagine what life would look like after this competition was over––so much had changed. I knew I was a water witch, I had a coven of sisters, and I was getting closer to the mystery surrounding my birth parents. The words of the lullaby Valerie had sung in my vision by the lake still echoed in my mind. *I know where I'm going/ And I know who's going with me/ I know who I love/ And the dear knows who I'll marry.* Where *would* I be going? Would I stay in my lovely cottage, continuing my career as a graphic designer? Would the secrets of my past that I was hoping to uncover change the course of my future, too? I'd always felt something missing in my life, not knowing anything about who my parents were. I mean, who left a baby in an apple box outside a bakery? Like I was a delivery of baking supplies. At least I knew I wasn't headed towards marriage—a husband was the last thing I needed to add to this messy equation.

But enough ruminating, Pops, I told myself. I had ingredients to collect and cakes to bake, and that deserved all of my attention right now. I pushed on.

CRAAAAAAAACK. *Crack, crack, crack.*

Gunfire shot through the air. Birds scattered, and my ears rang. Gateau mewed, and I picked her up and stroked her soft black fur. "Never mind that nasty earl and his hunting," I said to Gateau, who meowed back in agreement (or so I assumed). The gunshot was much louder than before; we must have gotten closer to the shooters. Gateau nuzzled into the crook of my arm, squashing her face into the sleeve of my linen shirt.

"Over here," a man's voice boomed from behind a huge bayberry bush.

"That must be the gamekeeper," I whispered to Gateau.

I went closer and peeked over the bush. Sure enough, the earl and the gamekeeper were bent over something on the ground. The body of some poor creature, no doubt. The earl lifted his head with the kind of delighted grin that made me realize I'd never seen a genuine smile from him before. He certainly looked pleased with himself.

The gamekeeper straightened, and I got my first proper look at his face. Like the earl, he was dressed in weirdly formal-looking hunting tweeds with knee-high brown boots, though his were more worn and beaten than those that belonged to his boss. He was perhaps ten years younger, too, with a tuft of still-brown hair peeking out from beneath a flat cap. His face was stern and set, but there was a softness around his crinkly brown eyes, and his shoulders gently sloped so as to make him look permanently humble. Suddenly, an image of him as a father playing with a young child popped into my brain. The vision surprised me. It wasn't the kind of thing I would have imagined thinking while looking at a man who was holding a shotgun. I shuddered. I hated guns, no matter what use they were being put to. I couldn't stomach the violence.

"Pick that up for me, Arthur," the earl instructed.

With a sigh, the gamekeeper picked up the dead bird, put it into a burlap bag, and then cocked his rifle so that it almost folded into two parts. I assumed the maneuver was the safety catch that Hamish had explained earlier so that you couldn't fire the rifle accidentally while walking.

"Aha, there's another one!" Lord Frome called out. He lifted his shotgun, clicked the two pieces back in place and raised the gun. There was a moment's silence, and I braced myself for the sound of gunfire, but then the earl lowered his weapon. "Little blighter was too fast. Next time."

The earl's words, combined with the sight of the weapon, gave me a cold feeling in my belly, and I decided to give both men a wide berth and find an alternative route to the farm.

Gateau jumped down from my arms, and we turned back the way we came. I spotted a little path that bordered the fields in the opposite direction I usually took. With any luck, it would bring me round to Susan's farm from the other side.

Gateau seemed more than happy to trot along, stopping every so often to poke her nose into the flowerbeds or to clean a paw. She was at home here, that was for sure, perhaps even more so than in my cottage in Norton St. Philip. For the first time, I seriously wondered what it might be like to leave my cottage and move to Broomewode Village. Would I be welcomed here? I'd spent so long making the Olde Bakery my home, painting the walls, filling it with furniture that suited its old beams and flagstone floor—I'd even managed to keep a few houseplants alive in its shady corners. And then there was Margaret, my irritable but adorable kitchen ghost. She'd seen me through days and days of baking, had prompted me in the right direction when I needed a guiding hand. What would become of Margaret if she couldn't have her daily chats with me? I watched as Gateau bounded ahead of me to chase a butterfly. If only she could talk and I could ask her advice.

We turned a corner, and a cottage came into view. I hadn't realized that anyone lived on this side of the grounds, but Broomewode Hall's grounds were so big, I probably hadn't explored half of the property. The cottage was adorable. It was wide and squat, the stone painted a pale cream, punctuated with little windows framed in black with lead piping crisscrossing the glass. A matching glossy black trim ran around the bottom of the cottage. I guessed it was a bungalow with rooms reaching farther back than I could see—a railroad structure, like my own cottage. It probably had a beautiful back garden. I closed my eyes for a moment, imagining blooming rose bushes—dusky pink and palest white. A huge deer antler was fixed over the front door, and I wondered whether this was the gamekeeper's cottage.

Muffled noises were coming from inside, which was strange considering the gamekeeper was out shooting. Perhaps my vision of him as a dad was true and he had a family. I stepped off the path onto the springy green lawn laid out like a halo around the cottage. I couldn't see if any lights were on inside, but I definitely heard voices. Gateau came to my side and mewed up at me. "Let's just take a quick look round the back," I whispered. She cocked her little head to the side as if to say, *Here we go again.*

I walked round the side of the cottage, and as I did, the muffled words became sharper and more distinct. "Sounds like someone's having an argument," I said to Gateau. I stopped by a side window. It was an argument all right, a nasty-sounding one, but the voices weren't the soft Somerset accent I'd come to expect from Broomewode villagers. The voices were American, with the rich round tones of one of the Southern states. Strange as it was, the voices sounded familiar. Was someone inside in trouble? Did they need my help?

"Now, now, Sue Ellen, just you get ahold of yourself," a male voice said.

Sue Ellen? I clapped my hand over my mouth to stifle a giggle. *Way to go, Pops. You've managed to reach new levels of silliness.*

I looked down at Gateau. "I don't think the cast of *Dallas* needs my help right now," I whispered, still laughing at myself. "Of course it was the TV. I'm the only American round here for miles." Whoever was inside was in the midst of a *Dallas* rerun.

But Gateau wasn't paying attention. Something had caught her canny kitten eye, and she was off—running round the side of the cottage. Great, like I needed a wild cat chase right now.

I had no choice but to follow her...right into grassland where she was chasing a baby grouse.

Instead of the beautiful back garden I'd imagined, behind the cottage were acres of green grass and rolling hills. It was a grouse moor, and several young grouse were wandering around. It was the first time I'd ever seen the birds up close, and they were extremely cute. Elegant heads with a small curved beak, gorgeous reddish feathers with brown speckles, a pear-shaped body on top of little webbed feet. How anyone could shoot these sweethearts? Well, they had a colder heart than me.

"Gateau," I whispered, "leave that poor thing alone." Gateau was skipping around a young grouse excitedly. Needless to say, my sweet familiar did not heed my words, but thankfully the mother grouse came and herded her young away from my kitten's beady eyes.

"Sorry," I said to the mother grouse. "She just wants to play."

I scooped up my kitty and stood away from the birds so that they'd know we meant them no harm.

"Let's get out of here before someone comes out and yells at us for being on their property," I said to Gateau, who let me know that she didn't appreciate her fun being ruined by not even raising her head in reply.

I rolled my eyes. If this is what motherhood was like, then it could definitely wait a few more years.

Back on the path, I put Gateau down and picked up my pace, looking forward to seeing Susan and catching up on the week's gossip. The sun emerged from behind a cloud, and the sudden warmth suffused my body. I rolled back the sleeves of my white linen shirt and readjusted the amethyst necklace Elspeth had given me. I touched the cool purple stone and felt thankful for its protection. We continued along the path, and I let my thoughts drift away from cakes and cottages and became absorbed in the nature around me.

I'd been walking in a half daze for about ten minutes when I realized I wasn't alone. Up ahead, a small group of people were gathered by the side of the woodland, several of them pointing at a tree. I stopped to take a closer look. The group looked to be an even split of men and women, all in various shades of beige and khaki, clothed in calico trousers and bucket hats. Several were clutching binoculars.

"Bird-watchers," I said to Gateau, who looked at me as if to say, *Yeah, tell me something I don't know.* I continued toward them and called out, "Hello." With perfect synchronicity, they all turned towards me, with the exception of one woman who was writing furiously in a notebook. Now that I was closer, they all seemed to be of retirement age, and they regarded me (and Gateau) with suspicion. "Lovely afternoon, isn't it?" I said cheerfully.

The woman with the notebook stopped writing and raised her head. "Not if you're a crow or a raven or even a magpie, it's not."

I stared at her for a moment, grasping for the right kind of response to her remark. She held my gaze, her gray eyes alert and inquiring. Despite the warm weather, she was wearing a fleece vest and a pair of expensive-looking binoculars hung about her neck. She was tall, perhaps almost six feet, with silver hair set in a manageable bob tucked behind her ears. She was still waiting for me to acknowledge her comment.

"Indeed," I managed to say, and with that, the group nodded in unison and turned their attention back to the tree.

I followed their gaze and saw two birds on a branch, seemingly in conversation with one another.

"It's a blackcap," the old woman said, looking at me with a hint of a smile playing about her lips. "Lovely, aren't they?"

"I'm not sure I've ever noticed one before," I confessed.

"You can easily identify them by their distinctive cap. This one on the right is a male. You can tell by his black cap, and he's talking to a lady—her cap is chestnut brown. Both have the same thin, dark-colored beaks and brownish-gray wings. A similar size to a robin, weighing in at around twenty-one grams."

Her tone was soft and kind, completely different from her earlier sharp comment. And hearing the loving way she spoke about the birds brought a smile to my face. There was nothing nicer than listening to someone speak about the things they felt passionate about. I watched the birds as they tweeted at each other.

"Marlene, we'd better push on," a man said.

Marlene. That was a nice name. I said goodbye and took the path away from the woodland towards the farm.

Before long, I turned off the woodchip path and onto Susan's long stone driveway, and soon the huge barn with its curved roof and the Somerset stone of the farmhouse came into view. As always, the fragrant, earthy scent of the herb garden filled my nostrils, and as I turned to Gateau to remark on its gorgeousness, I saw that she'd disappeared, which could only mean one thing. And there he was!

Sly's red ball rolled towards my feet, and I giggled as his mass of black and white fur bounded over. Always happy to oblige, I picked up the slobbery ball and threw it as far as I could along the path. It soared into the sky. "Wow, I'm getting good at that," I said to Sly's fluffy behind as he galloped after the red blur. As I watched its trajectory, I spotted the now-familiar silhouette of a hawk as it glided along the treetops. Could it really be the same one as earlier? And if so, was it trying to tell me something? I should have asked the bird-watchers if they'd seen a hawk, or a flock of hawks, and what drew them to certain areas.

I probably would have gotten lost in hawkish thoughts,

but thankfully Sly brought back his ball for another throw. And I obliged, of course.

"Hello there, Poppy," Susan called, leaning out of the window of her kitchen.

I waved and said I'd be inside as soon as I'd sated Sly's ball obsession. She laughed and said in that case, she'd see me next week.

I threw the ball a couple more times and then promised we could play more later. Sly seemed to understand and followed as I went round to the side door and into the kitchen.

Susan stood by the stove, pouring a kettle of boiling water into a teapot. She was wearing a pair of navy-blue jodhpurs and a matching oversize tank top with a few stray stems of green stuck to the hem.

"Hello, Poppy. I thought I'd treat you to some dandelion tea," she said, smiling.

Hmmm, I wasn't so sure that was a treat, but I accepted a cup and saucer and followed Susan's command to sit at the kitchen table.

"It's an ancient recipe," she said. "Packed full of iron. Very healing. And it'll keep your strength up, too. This batch is from the garden, of course. It's made from the flower petals, so it's sweet and delicate."

I blew across the liquid's hot surface and took a hesitant sip. But Susan was right. It was sweet and a little earthy with a slight medicinal quality that was actually quite nice. I told her as much, and she laughed that throaty chuckle of hers. She settled in the chair opposite me, and Sly went and sat by her feet. She tickled behind his ear, and he flopped his head onto her feet.

I asked Susan about her week, and she talked about the pressures of the farm but that she was happy to be busy. Reg had been over in the week, and she'd cooked a new recipe: venison stew with dumplings. "It was lovely with the bottle of Barolo he brought." She flushed a little at the memory. "He keeps a little cellar, and he exchanges vintages with the earl sometimes."

"I saw the earl and one of his gamekeepers, Arthur, earlier. They were out shooting 'vermin.' I think the whole thing's a bit icky. Those outfits they wear and those brutal shotguns. " I shuddered.

"Oh, yes. It's that time of year, I suppose. I agree that it seems very unnecessary to kill the wild birds so that he's got more grouse to shoot during hunting season."

I described the group of bird-watchers I'd come across. "There were about eight in total, mostly older women and men, all wearing bucket hats and carrying binoculars."

"Sounds like you met the local members of the Somerset Wild Bird Protection Society."

I remarked that it was strange I'd never seen them walking around Broomewode before.

"They travel through the area a lot, visiting different places of interest. They might be a bit older, but they're extremely active, and they really have it in for the earl."

I raised an eyebrow and took another sip of herbal tea. "Tell me more," I said, intrigued. Was there anyone round here who actually liked the earl?

"Well, they believe that Lord Frome takes his right to protect his flock of game birds a little too far. A blood sport, they call it. In fact, I'm sure I have their brochure somewhere around here. They post them out every couple of months or so with details of conservation aims, indoor talks, local bird-watching trips and...well, honestly, I'm afraid I never get past the first couple of pages." She laughed. "Far too much to do around the farm."

Susan went into the hallway, and I heard her rummaging through some drawers, muttering about needing to do a big clear-out. She returned after a minute or so, brandishing a wad of papers.

"Here," she said, passing me a couple of brochures. "There's more than I thought. I can't tell if they want me to join them or if they think I'm an evil farmer running around shooting anything that moves."

The brochure was thick and glossy, a multi-colored bird I'd never seen before on the front cover along with the words: *The Somerset Wild Bird Protection Society: Spring Newsletter.* I flicked through the pages to their mission statement and learned that the society had been running for over a hundred years. They were committed to furthering the study of birds in the country and to assist in their preservation. There were two hundred members, and their aim was to appeal to anyone interested in the birds of Somerset, and to preserve the local birdlife. Next to the statement was a series of photographs of their members out walking with binoculars and notebooks. I spotted Marlene, the woman I'd spoken to earlier, immediately. She was wearing the same hat and was looking to the left of the camera with the same stern expression she'd given me. She obviously had an important role in the society.

When I looked up, Susan was regarding me curiously. "I didn't peg you for a bird-watcher," she said.

"I'm not, but I'm glad someone's looking out for the wild birds."

"I donate money to them when I can. They're a stubborn bunch, doing good work. But I have to do it secretly, of course, since I'm a tenant of the earl's."

"I guess that wouldn't go down so well if he found out you were funding them, huh, what with his passion for hunting."

Susan nodded and suddenly looked serious. "Be careful while the earl's out with his shotgun. He seems to shoot first and ask questions later."

CHAPTER 3

I left Susan's with a basket laden with farm goods. Six happy eggs, an enormous punnet of strawberries, and beautiful sprigs of fresh basil from the herb garden. The basil was bright green and incredibly fragrant. I was hopeful that the fruit and herb combination would come together and make my cake stand out from the rest. Susan also gifted me a few perfectly shaped figs, suggesting that I slice the fruit into wedges and use them as decoration around the base of my layer cake. It was a great idea; the purple color would make the basil-tinged cream and macerated strawberries pop.

I was so grateful to my coven sister Susan for all the special farm ingredients she supplied. Preparing for this competition had taught me a lot about the value of using local produce. Obviously, getting your ingredients locally meant that they were likely to be fresher. In my case, they were literally going "from farm to table" or "the judging table," I should say. There was no travel time, unlike produce that was imported, so my ingredients were as fresh as could possibly be, with no need for preservatives, and the fruit had had enough time to ripen. Not to mention how I knew for sure that no pesticides had been used on the crops. This meant no compromise on flavor—but also aesthetics. My fruit and herbs were fresh and pretty to boot, and every tiny bit of advantage helped this late in the competition.

It was also a lot kinder to the environment to use local produce. Less energy had been used for harvesting (although Susan would probably disagree; it took a lot of her personal energy to keep the farm running!). And there was also no need to use fuel to transport the goods anywhere. Susan sold most of her crops in local shops, which could be delivered by one of her helpers in an old white van with Broomewode Farm painted onto the side in blue. This also meant that the local economy was supported. Small gift shops like the one in the village relied on the appeal of local produce to sell to tourists.

I'd been so busy mentally extolling the virtues of Susan's farm, I'd almost missed the turning to get back to the competition tent. Luckily, Gateau meowed and turned right, letting me know just how dozy she thought her owner was.

"Thank you, sweet thing," I said to her swishing behind. "These strawberries need to be refrigerated before the June sunshine turns them soft."

Following in Gateau's paw-steps, I happily made my way back to the tent to deliver my ingredients to the safety of *The Great British Baking Contest's* fridges. Despite the pressure, I was looking forward to filming. I was confident that my head was in the game this week. I'd made it so much further than I'd anticipated, and the glory of last week's win was still coursing through my veins.

I heard panting behind me and turned to see Sly bounding down the path, red ball wedged between his teeth.

"Oh, Sly!" I laughed. "Are you escorting me back to the tent? Aren't I the lucky one to have not one, but two special creatures deliver me to my destination?"

At this, Gateau let out an aggravated meow. I bent down as I whispered into her ear, "Of course, you're my number one. Sly belongs to Susan, and you're my very special familiar."

None the wiser, Sly barked happily and dropped the ball at my feet. I obliged, of course, and threw the ball high into the air. I had to admit, my aim was getting better. If only I'd had Sly around while I was practicing for the softball team in high school, maybe I would have become a famous athlete. And to my surprise, Gateau didn't do her usual *see dog and run* routine. She stayed right by me, raising her little nose into the air to show everyone who was boss, her amble turning into a strut. "Are you getting used to your canine brother?" I murmured. She shot me a look of pure disgust. "Okay, okay, I'm sorry. That was a step too far."

Sly came running back, but to my surprise, he didn't drop the ball at my feet again, ready for another go. Instead he kept the slobbery thing and took up position next to me on the opposite side to Gateau. I grinned. Flanked between these two, I felt invincible. *Team Poppy reporting for duty.*

The pond was up ahead, and two swans came into view, their long, elegant necks held high, pristine white features gliding along with no indication of how hard their webbed feet were pedaling through the water. Come to think of it, filming the show was a lot like being a swan. Contestants had to come across as composed and graceful, in control of their mixers and ovens—even like they were having a good time. But beneath the surface was a manic inner swan, desperately trying to remember the right order of their complicated cake method, to not forget the sugar or flour, to get enough air into the mix for a light and fluffy batter. I gave the swans a small nod as I passed. We were kindred spirits.

I paused for a moment to appreciate the gardens, the fine display of flowers and shrubs, inhaling the scent of magnolias again, which were growing by a yew hedge.

"Keee-eeeee-arr."

A hoarse screech careened through the air. I looked up. There was the hawk again, soaring by the treetops. Was he signaling to another hawk? Perhaps there was a flock of them in Broomewode, but until last week, I'd never seen these magnificent birds in Somerset before. Was it mating season? If only I'd asked the bird-watching group when I'd had the opportunity. If I passed them on my way back to the tent, I'd stop them and see what they knew.

The hawk let out another shrill call. I paused and shielded my eyes from the sun to watch his graceful flight. His wingspan was so impressive—speckled feathers spread out to make a wide, majestic fan, head angled forward in concentration, focused on something I couldn't see. "What a beauty," I said to the sky.

I could have stared at him for hours, but out of the corner of my eye, something glinted in the sun. As I turned, I heard the cock of a shotgun, and to my horror, I saw the earl pointing his gun at the hawk. I was stunned, momentarily paralyzed by what I was seeing. Surely he wasn't...couldn't actually be... Before I could engage my thoughts with my mouth and scream out "NO," Sly growled, dropped his ball and ran towards the earl. Gateau followed suit, and the two raced side by side until Sly reached the earl's feet and nipped his ankles and Gateau took a running jump and scaled his back.

Go get him, girl!

With all my strength, I opened my mouth and yelled at the earl. "Stop! Put that gun down!"

But there was an almighty blast, and gunshot sounded through the air.

I held my breath as I looked up. But between them, Sly and Gateau had thrown the earl's aim, and the hawk disappeared into the woodland. I let out a sigh of relief. Thank goodness for those two scamps. They'd saved that beautiful wild bird. Seriously good teamwork for a rival cat and dog.

But the earl did not share my joy. Gateau jumped down and joined Sly as they scampered back to my side. I saw now that the earl's gamekeeper, Arthur, was behind his boss, confusion and irritation on his face.

The earl stomped over to me, red and sweaty, veins bulging in his forehead. "You need to mind your own business, young lady," he barked, any pretense at being the convivial Lord of the Manor now fully dissipated. "I have every right to shoot vermin polluting my own land. And get those animals away from me." He looked down at his trouser leg, aggressively brushing a few of Sly's hairs from the fabric.

As he continued to tell me to keep my "beasts" under control, he began to wave his shotgun about, brandishing it in my direction as if *I* was one of the vermin polluting his property. Charming. I felt the telltale signs of indignation prick along the small of my back, and I drew myself up to full height, preparing to defend myself, my familiars, and the good of all earthly creatures far and wide.

But before I could launch into a tirade of my own, another man came running over the hill and into view. Oh great. More hunters. But I was ready to stand my ground, no matter how many men with guns showed up.

To my surprise, the running man was Benedict. No gun in hand, just a pair of gardening shears. He was wearing the same outfit I'd seen him gardening in before: an old flannel shirt with grass strains, heavy work trousers with frayed hems, toolbelt around the waist. He was sweating and out of breath as if he'd run a sprinting race.

He stopped and looked hard at me and then at his father, obviously perplexed. It was rare for me to see father and son side by side, and the resemblance was striking. High foreheads, long, straight noses, and that chin that lent them both an imperious edge.

"I heard a woman screaming," Benedict finally spluttered. "I thought someone was in trouble."

The earl's arm shot out, and he pointed at me accusingly. "The shrieking voice belongs to your friend Miss Wilkinson here," the earl said.

"Your father tried to shoot a hawk," I said, turning to Benedict. "A hawk," I repeated. "Which I'm pretty darned sure isn't on his list of"—here I stopped and air-quoted —"pest species."

To my relief (and his credit), Benedict looked at his father in horror. "Father, it's nesting season now. You could be fined or even go to jail for killing a hawk."

At that, the gamekeeper, Arthur, burst into laughter. "I can't quite see that happening, can you?"

The earl matched his laughter, which to my ears sounded so superior. Like this was feudal times and he was untouchable.

When Benedict didn't join in the laughter, the earl stopped and said, with a sneer in his tone, "I was aiming at a raven, but this woman and her pets attacked me and threw off my aim. Arthur was here the whole time. He saw what happened."

"Indeed," Arthur said, explaining that he'd witnessed the whole scene. "It was definitely a raven. The young lady's not from these parts. She doesn't know the local birds."

My jaw fell open. I knew what I'd seen, and I wasn't going to be bullied by two entitled men. Right now, I had no way to prove that bird had been a hawk, but now that I knew they were protected, I'd be doing everything in my power to save that beautiful bird. I wasn't sure why, but I felt a bond, almost a kinship with the hawk.

CHAPTER 4

*B*y the time I arrived back at the competition tent, my optimistic mood had been shattered and I felt flustered and annoyed. Lord Frome might be the King of the Castle of this small pocket of Somerset, but that didn't give him carte blanche to treat the landscape and wildlife as his own personal playground. Even though I should have expected bad behavior from the earl by now, I was disappointed by his cruelty—and I really didn't appreciate being spoken to like I was an interfering, foolish woman. The way the gamekeeper backed up his boss with such a blatant lie made my blood boil. More than anything, I wanted to show those two men that they couldn't steamroll me. I was going to prove that the earl was engaging in illegal hunting.

I felt a strong urge to call my dad in the South of France. When I was growing up, he'd taught me the importance of respecting the local wildlife when we'd gone on camping trips. He explained how to only forage what we needed from woodland, which mushrooms would be delicious fried in a dollop of rich butter on the camp stove and which ones would cause a trip to the ER. He'd showed me how to safely start a fire with flint stones, how to keep it crackling with the right amount of dry twigs. I'd love to hear his soothing voice right now, let him tell me that people get their just deserts in one way or another: The universe had its own way of making sure that happened so we didn't need to intervene. He was so sanguine. I don't know how he managed to stay calm all the time, but I needed to take a leaf out of his horticulture book, so to speak.

So I took a few deep breaths and then approached the tent, where Martin, the new security guard Florence had made her latest target, was manning the entrance.

He held up one hand to stop me. "I'm afraid this part of the grounds is off-limits to the general public," he said.

I laughed and pointed to my basket of ingredients, lifting the terry cloth towel to show him my impressive stash. "I'm not the general public. I'm on the show."

He shook his head. "Filming doesn't begin until tomorrow morning."

Was this guy for real? "I was here this morning, with Hamish and Florence—two other contestants. We were putting our ingredients away, but I had to go and collect the rest of mine from the farm."

"I don't recall seeing you, miss," he said.

Go figure. All his attention had obviously been on Florence and her mane of chestnut curls.

Out of the corner of my eye, I saw Fiona, the director, pacing while talking on the phone by the side of the tent. "I'll get Fiona to vouch for me, shall I?" I said, striding off in somewhat of a huff, my already stormy mood darkening further.

As I got closer to Fiona, I could see that she wasn't going to be too impressed by my interrupting her call. Whatever it was she was discussing, it looked heated, and deep frown lines furrowed her forehead.

But these strawberries needed refrigerating, and no security guard with a selective memory was going to stop that from happening.

I approached with caution and waited to catch her eye. "Excuse me," I mouthed, suddenly meek at the prospect of being a nuisance to the show's director. "But I need your help."

She looked at me with exasperation as if to say, *Darling, clearly you need more help than I could give you.* But to my surprise, she said, "I'll call you back" into her cell phone and hung up.

I explained my predicament, and she sighed heavily before walking back to the entrance with me.

"Martin, this is Poppy Wilkinson. She's a contestant on the show. And she was here about an hour ago. Which you should have noticed, if you were doing your job."

Martin turned pale.

"It's all very well being vigilant against trespassers," Fiona continued, "but you mustn't chase away the bakers or we'll have no show."

I suddenly felt very bad for Martin, who, after all, was new and just trying to do a good job. He looked deflated. "Can't be too careful," he murmured, and Fiona walked off, no doubt to get back to whoever was stressing her on the end of that phone call.

I felt bad for Fiona. The crew worked so hard. I couldn't even imagine being the one to call the shots on set. She had to make split-second decisions for the good of the show on a minute-by-minute basis, with multiple cameras and inexperienced contestants. I mean, it was exhausting for us baking for up to four and half hours straight, but imagine being forced to watch us flapping about the tent, stirring and huffing and trying not to sweat into the flour mix, and turning it all into a compelling narrative.

Finally back inside the tent and putting my ingredients away, I took in the bustle still going on. The crew were amazing. Between them all, each week they told the story of each bake from beginning to end, the ups and downs, and the judges' reactions. They were capturing our personalities minute by minute, building up our story. And so far, we'd been pretty lucky with the weather. Only once had we had to stop for a heavy rain. All that water thundering on the calico roof of the tent had been a nightmare for Robbie and the other sound technicians. I watched as the gaffers checked the lights and electrics, and the drone operator prepared to take some aerial footage. I wondered if the earl would shoot the drone out of the sky and claim it was a magpie.

Donald Friesen, the series producer, had told us that it was like an avalanche when the cameras start rolling. There was no stopping the process. "It's more like a documentary," he'd said before the show began filming, "freewheeling and flowing—we have to follow where the action is but without stepping on any of the bakers' toes." Now that I'd been doing this for a while, I knew what he meant. Often, a camera might be trained on you while you slipped your cake into the oven, when suddenly a disaster would be happening on the farthest bench and the crew would rush to catch it.

I closed the door to the fridge, said a quick hello to the data wrangler, and waved at the crew members I was getting to know. I hoped everyone could feel how grateful I was for all their hard work. It was the crew who were making my dream come true minute by minute.

TIME HAD GOTTEN AWAY from me, and when I arrived back at the pub, Hamish and Florence were already tucking into dessert. I don't know how those two managed to have a sweet tooth during filming. Florence caught my eye, gestured down at her cake, and sighed. "You've got to try this rum and walnut cake. It's incredible. Darius recommended it, or I'd never have been able to face another bite of cake. It's all I've eaten all week as I've been practicing."

I took the seat next to her and slipped my arm around her shoulders, squeezing her gently. "I know. But you're going to be fantastic."

Hamish nodded. "You're giving us a run for our money, that's for sure." He took a final bite of apple cake. "There's a new cake and pastry chef in the kitchen. She's a wizard." Florence fed me a bite of her cake, and it was so good, I was relieved the magician in the kitchen wasn't in the baking competition. I also realized I was famished. It was time to refuel and keep my strength up, as Elspeth always advised me to do.

Darius, the gorgeous new barman, hovered by our table,

sending hot glances Florence's way. She sent some pretty hot ones back.

Sorry, buddy, I thought, catching his eye and smiling, *you'll have to do with me for now*. Darius whipped out his order pad and told me that the lunch special was hot smoked salmon quiche with a watercress salad.

"Sold," I said, smiling again. "And a side of fries?"

"Save room for cake," Florence reminded me. Oh, dear. Was I being greedy? But who could resist french fries? Especially with a pot of homemade aioli. Well, at least the earl and his shooting antics hadn't put me off my food.

Florence poured me a glass of sparkling water from the bottle on the table and I drank it down, still smarting from my run-in with the earl. Maybe Hamish would know about hunting laws, especially the ones the earl and his gamekeeper were bending to their personal whims.

I related to Florence and Hamish what had happened on the way back from Susan's farm, describing how Sly and Gateau (now both off doing their regular animal duties— herding for Sly, napping for Gateau) instinctively pounced on the earl as he tried to take down a hawk, throwing his aim.

"He said that it's within his rights to eliminate so-called vermin from his land," I continued, "but surely that can't extend to birds of prey?"

As I spoke, I could feel the earlier indignation rise up through my chest, making my heart pound. How dare he try to take down such a majestic bird? What entitlement. What ignorance.

"Poppy," Florence said, "you're turning the most terrific shade of pink. If only I could get my cheeks to flush that way naturally, I'd shave off a good fifteen minutes from my morning routine."

I giggled. Florence knew exactly how to dissipate a bad vibe, and I took a few deep breaths. But jokes aside, this was a serious matter. Benedict had suggested his father could go to jail for killing certain birds during mating season. I turned to Hamish. "Do you know what the law says about this?"

Hamish nodded and placed his fork back on his plate. "Well, there's something called the Wildlife and Countryside Act. It was formed in 1981 to protect animals, plants and certain habitats here in the UK. I know a bit about it from raising my Shetland ponies and trying to live as peacefully on my land as possible. It definitely protects all wild birds, so any species which lives in the wild, but it doesn't extend to game birds, which are protected by the game act when it's not hunting season."

I sat forward in my chair. "So a hawk should fall under that act, right?"

"Yes. It's one of the basic laws that no person should intentionally kill, injure, or remove any wild bird from their natural habitat."

I let out my breath and relaxed into my chair again. "But wait, aren't ravens wild birds?"

"Remember, landowners are allowed to shoot certain pest species, including ravens. It helps to regulate the natural cycle of wildlife, plus it keeps the grouse and pheasant plentiful for shooting season. But there's not much we can do if the earl denies aiming for the hawk."

I felt irritated, but I was also an outsider. I couldn't understand why the natural world would need our help to regulate itself, but I trusted Hamish, and if he said it was acceptable, then I wasn't going to argue. Chatting with Susan about the farm had demonstrated how farmers needed to be tough and had a much more no-nonsense approach to life and death on the land than I knew how to stomach.

I would have pressed the matter further, but Darius returned with my quiche. "And here are your fries," he said, placing them next to my plate.

"Efcharistó," Florence said, throwing back her hair and showing off those perfect white teeth.

She could speak Greek? I was impressed all over again.

"Parakaló," Darius replied, gazing soulfully at Florence.

Er, this was my lunch. Could I get in a word of thanks, please?

I thanked Darius, in English, and sliced into the quiche. It was warm and firm, the egg and salmon a perfect combination, and the pastry was flaky and buttery. The watercress was a great accompaniment to the rich quiche—peppery and crisp. So refreshing. I sighed with satisfaction and dipped a fry into the garlicky aioli.

Florence asked Hamish more about his farm and how he looked after Shetland ponies. As he talked, I realized I wasn't the only one spinning plates to be on this show. Not only did Hamish have all that land to look after, he also had a full-time job as a police officer *and* he baked. I had so much respect for how hard he worked.

I looked around the pub to see if Eve was working. As usual, it was busy with lunch trade, most of the oak tables were filled with groups of laughing friends and families gathering to mark the end of the working week. I spotted Eve in the corner of the bar, pouring a pint of cider from the tap for a tall gentleman. I squinted. I knew the back of that head.

I quickly polished off the rest of my lunch, trying not to scald the roof of my mouth scoffing hot fries, and then interrupted Hamish and Florence's sibling-like back-and-forth to excuse myself for a moment. "I'm going to demand some answers," I said and grabbed a last fry as I headed to the bar.

I tapped the man on the shoulder. "Benedict," I said, "I'd love to have a quick chat with you."

He turned slowly and greeted me with an expression of wry amusement. He'd changed out of his worn flannel shirt and now had on a smart, button-down blue Oxford shirt with dark jeans. "Hello again, Poppy," he said, a small smile flickering at the corners of his lips.

That hint of a smile made my blood boil. Was he laughing at me for saving a beautiful wild creature from his gun-crazed father? I decided to let him have it.

"You know that your father almost broke the law today, right? He tried to shoot a beautiful hawk. He tried to gun it down mid-flight."

Benedict frowned, all hint of playfulness gone in a flash. "I was there, Poppy. And if my father says he wasn't aiming at the hawk, then I believe him. What you're accusing him of is a very serious matter. As serious as falsely accusing someone of breaking the law. You may have been quite the detective around these parts the last few weeks, but even you should know that you need evidence to make such an accusation."

I swallowed. Benedict could be very imposing when he wanted, switching to a haughty, superior tone in a flash. But I knew what I'd seen. I had to stick to my convictions and maybe change tack a little.

In a softer voice, I said, "I was there, Benedict. I saw him aim at that hawk. It was why Gateau and Sly ambushed him."

He raised one brow, and I noticed a smudge of dirt, probably soil, on the left side of his forehead. "Gateau and Sly?"

Despite myself, I lost some of my righteous indignation. "My cat and Susan Bentley's border collie."

He smiled again, his stern face softening. "It's quite an adorable sight, you walking around the village with a kitten and a herding dog."

I was still annoyed, but it was nice to know that I looked adorable and not like I'd lost my marbles. *Adorable.* I let my mind linger on the word for a moment.

"But Poppy, listen. I understand your concern. But if my father denies he was aiming at a hawk and Arthur backs him up, what can I do? They're within their rights to control vermin on the land."

I shook my head, recalling how Benedict had charged up the hill in his gardening gear, out of breath, worried that he'd heard a woman yelling. I couldn't deny that his heart was in the right place.

"I noticed you weren't carrying a shotgun. Don't you accompany your father on his hunting expeditions?"

Benedict paused for a moment, seeming to weigh up his response. "It's not really my thing."

"Don't like shooting with your father?" And who could blame him?

"To tell you the truth, I hate the idea of killing living beings."

At that, I instantly softened. They might have a striking physical resemblance, but Benedict and Lord Frome were nothing alike in spirit. "I'm glad."

"Well, it makes me odd man out around here. What can I

do?" he continued. "It's the way of the land around here. My father is simply adhering to tradition."

Before I could respond, Susan came into the pub and joined us at the bar. She told me that she was meeting Reginald for *a spot of lunch,* as she put it. I still wasn't used to many funny British sayings. Benedict took this as his cue to escape, and after bidding Susan a nice afternoon, nodded to me and left.

Eve came over, leaned over the bar, and greeted Susan with a peck on the cheek. "What did you say to young Champney?" Eve asked, a teasing tone to her voice. "I've never seen a man leave a pub so quickly." She tossed her long, gray braid over one shoulder and chuckled.

Thanks, Eve. Way to make me feel like a man-repeller.

"I think confronting him about his dad's hunting habit sent him over the edge," I confessed.

I told the two women the same story I'd just recounted to Florence and Hamish, except this time I could explain, in a low voice to two of my witch sisters, that Sly had probably followed me down the path because he sensed that I was in danger.

At that, Susan beamed. "He's such a good familiar. A heart of pure gold. But the earl has a heart of stone. What a monster."

Eve agreed, her kind, clear eyes misting over with anger. I went on to describe the majesty of the hawk, his graceful swoop through the clear blue skies. I knew my coven sisters would understand the beauty of the animal kingdom. "What's funny is that I'm sure I've seen the same hawk three times now. He appeared last week, circling the Orangery before that fated wedding." I bowed my head at the memory.

"Does that sound crazy? I mean, how many hawks could there really be in this sleepy village? It was like he knew I was coming."

Eve looked reflective and smoothed down the tan apron tied around her waist. "It doesn't sound crazy. It sounds like there's a connection between you and the hawk. I don't think it was coincidence that you appeared just as the earl spotted his next victim."

I sank onto the barstool. It was a relief to hear that Susan and Eve didn't think I'd lost the plot, but why were the hawk and I connected? It didn't make sense.

Eve sensed my confusion. "It's a full moon tonight, Poppy, remember? The coven will be gathering—we can put it to them. The power of the circle is much stronger than the power of a single witch."

What with preparing for this week's competition, I *had* forgotten that a magic circle was meeting tonight. I nodded fiercely. "That's a great idea."

"And perhaps we'll try to both ruin the earl's aim and protect that hawk," Susan added. "Two birds, no stone," she joked.

"But do you have any ideas why I keep seeing the same hawk?" I asked.

"It could be your spirit guide," Eve replied.

Susan nodded. "Also, think about what a hawk symbolizes. It's associated with good luck, clarity, and rising above bad situations so you can see the big picture. It's also a bird of war. That means you're in a struggle right now, but you will prevail."

I did feel like I was in a struggle. It was a battle every week to do well enough in my baking to get to the next round, and then there was the struggle to find out more about my own history. I had begun my life here at Broomewode, and somehow I felt that my destiny was also here.

I was determined to do everything I could to protect that hawk. Maybe it was only a symbol, but it was a powerful and personal one to me. I told them I'd be there that night for the magic circle.

"Looks like Team Poppy has yet another member."

I spun round, and there was Gerry. For a split second, I toyed with the idea of telling my coven sisters about my special gift, but perhaps a magical hawk was enough for one day.

I shot Gerry a subtle signal that I'd meet him upstairs. Then Reginald arrived and swept Susan off to a cozy corner, and Eve accompanied them with a bottle of wine. I did enjoy how those two indulged in a little lunchtime luxury.

"That must be why I'm here, Pops," Gerry said, puffing out his chest and looking very important. "I'm your spirit guide."

I slipped off the barstool, told Florence and Hamish I was going to do some recipe book reading, and gestured to Gerry to follow me back to my room. At least this time I was inviting Gerry upstairs, rather than finding him lounging on my bed when I arrived at the inn.

I closed the door firmly behind me (no way was I going to get busted talking to thin air) and regarded Gerry.

"My spirit guide?" I said, rolling my eyes. "How can you be my spirit guide? You haven't even figured out how to be a proper spirit yet."

He pouted. "No need to be so mean, Pops. I'm working on some new tricks. In fact"—he began to levitate, feet lifting up from the floor and then pointing to the ceiling as he executed a perfect tumble turn—"watch this."

"Okay." But before Gerry could try to wow me, a screechy meow signaled the entrance of Gateau as she scampered through the open window. She landed on my bed and hissed at Gerry.

"Oh no, not you again," Gerry said, staring down my sweet familiar and floating back down. "You've thrown my concentration completely."

"You two need to learn to get along," I said. "But if you can't show me your new trick now, I'll show you mine. Here's a little something I've been working on this week," I said, in the rehearsed voice I used when the cameras were trained on me during the baking competition.

I closed my eyes and settled myself before opening them again and training them on the key to the door, which was still snug in the lock. I felt a huge energy surge rushing up from the balls of my feet and through my body.

I pictured the key turning in the lock, and without being quite aware I was doing it, my wrist rotated and my fingers mimicked rotating a key.

Earth, water, fire and air,
Help me to get from here to there.
Open this lock, let my wish be the key.
As I will, so mote it be.

My focus was absolute, and it didn't waver until I heard the key turn in the lock. "Ta-da!" I said, pleased with myself. This was my first time achieving that spell with an audience other than Gateau.

"Impressive," Gerry said.

46

Then I turned it back again, very satisfied when I heard the click of the lock.

I grinned and opened my eyes. "I can lock and unlock doors now. How neat is that?"

But Gerry had complimented me as much as he was going to. Arms folded across his chest, he said, "Well, I can go right through a door." And that's exactly what he did.

CHAPTER 5

J sat at my window and watched night fall, the sun slowly sinking into the horizon, yellow turning into orange into pink and finally disappearing. In its place, the moon rose, casting the rolling hills of Broomewode in a silver glow. A stack of recipe books sat beside me, abandoned, as I lost myself in thoughts about the hawk, my birth mom, and the little information I had about my birth dad. Gateau napped on my feet, and I stroked her soft, black fur, her gentle purrs a soothing accompaniment to my musings.

The minute the sky turned the blue-black of true night, I gently extricated myself from my position as Gateau's pillow, buttoned a chunky cardigan over my shirt and slipped on my sneakers. I'd wound my hair into a high bun earlier, and as I stared at my reflection in the bathroom mirror, I deliberated about whether to add a pair of hoops to my ensemble before chastising myself. Florence's fashionista voice had clearly wormed its way into my psyche. *It's a magic circle, not a fashion show, Pops.*

I left the inn through the back door, making sure to stay

out of sight from any of the other contestants who'd arrived after the working day had finished. Although I'd love to see Gaurav, Maggie, and the others, I didn't want to draw any attention to myself. I'd already gained a reputation for wandering off and getting involved in the village drama, and I certainly didn't want to encourage any more speculation. I imagined kindly Maggie lowering her glasses and asking where a young lady was off to by herself in the dark. And it wasn't like I could reply, *Oh, just on my way to a magic circle to join forces with my coven of witches.*

Outside, it was chillier than I'd imagined while I'd been cozying up with Gateau, and I was glad of the extra layer. I followed the narrow pebbled path lit by old-fashioned caged lanterns, its rows of whitebeam trees rising up either side of me, their puffy leaves swaying gently in the breeze. I recalled when Elspeth had accompanied me to my first circle a few short weeks ago. So much had happened since then. I was looking forward to seeing Elspeth Peach, contest judge and my witchy godmother, and hoped that she'd be able to help me get to the bottom of my mystery hawk.

I stopped for a moment, looking back in the direction of the inn and the manor house, and gasped. There was a shadowy figure in the distance. My heart began to beat rapidly. Who was that? I squinted and realized the figure was coming closer. *Okay, Pops, stay calm. It's definitely not an ax-murderer on the loose, probably just someone walking off their dinner.* I stayed rooted to the spot. Was it better to keep walking? Pretend I hadn't seen anything? But the decision was taken out of my hands when a bright light flashed in my face. I blinked rapidly, one, two, three times, then put my hand in front of my eyes.

"Oh, sorry, miss," a man's voice said. "Didn't mean to blind you there. Just doing my rounds."

The bright spots cleared themselves from my eyes, and there was Martin, the new security guard from the competition tent. He was still in uniform, and a walkie-talkie was strapped to his belt.

"Oh," I said, bemused as to what he was doing so far from the tent. I'd never seen any security straying so far from their base. Was he onto me? Did he know I was off to do some magic?

"I'm fine," I said quickly. "Couldn't settle before filming starts tomorrow, so thought I'd have a short stroll around the grounds."

Martin frowned. "Well, please do be careful, Miss...."

"Wilkinson. Call me Poppy."

"Poppy, then," he said, smiling. "It's a lovely, clear evening, but you never can be too careful."

That seemed to be Martin's catchphrase.

He wished me a nice evening and turned back towards the inn. I let out my breath. To get through the weekend, I'd have to stop jumping to the conclusion that a murderer was on the loose each time I bumped into someone. I rolled my shoulders a few times, shook out my hands, and continued along the path that would take me into the woods and the magic circle. If I remembered correctly, I'd have to climb a short hill and then through a smattering of thick trees before I'd reach the clearing.

As I walked, I concentrated on the image of the hawk soaring, trying to recall exactly where and when I'd spotted him. Did each sighting have something in common? Why didn't I pay more attention? Surely by now I should have figured out that every small detail counted. I was letting my sleuthing side down.

Before long, I came out into the clearing with its circle of standing stones reminiscent of those at Stonehenge, except on a much smaller scale. One big headstone loomed over the rest, and a few others had fallen over and were badly weathered. The ancient stones were protected by law, but in earlier times, people used to break the massive stones up to build houses and fences. Now there were gaps in the circle, and that's where I spotted Eve, Susan, and Elspeth. I immediately felt calm and ready to hear their plan. If only I could bottle this feeling of contentment I felt around them, I'd be a cracking witch *and* a millionaire.

"Poppy dearest," Elspeth said. "Blessed be. Welcome back. It's so good to see you." She delicately touched my hand, and I felt the familiar ZING race through me. Other women approached me, took my hands and repeated the same greeting. I smiled at each one warmly, my heart full. I looked up at the gorgeous moon and silently thanked it for bringing me and these women together this evening. The very air felt sacred and special, and I took deep lungfuls, feeling myself revived with each breath. Tonight I would get answers.

I looked around. Seven other members of the Broomewode Coven were present, including the older lady who'd first called me Valerie and her daughter. I was surprised that Jonathon wasn't present, but there was no time to ask questions, as Elspeth was already giving Eve the go-ahead to begin proceedings.

Eve took huge candles and placed them in a circle within the stones. As before, she looked to Elspeth before making another move. With a graceful swoop of her hands, Elspeth made a circling motion with her outstretched finger, and each of the candles sprang to light, one after another, like delicate fairy lights. Although I hadn't seen anyone light incense, the distinctive spiced smell of patchouli entered into the air. The atmosphere felt electric.

"Sisters," Elspeth said, looking at each of us in turn, "we are gathered here tonight to pay our respects and show gratitude to another full moon passing. We will also work to protect the spirits of the air."

I smiled at Eve, grateful that she'd already passed on the message about the hawk to Elspeth. And, with no disrespect to Jonathon, I felt comforted by being in a circle of only women. My sisters.

Susan took my left hand; one of the Broomewode cooks whose name I didn't know took my right; and just like that, the circle began. A gentle ripple of electricity began in my fingertips, and then waves of fizzing energy weaved through my forearms and into my chest. I still hadn't gotten used to this strange sensation. It was powerful but not overwhelming, a force that helped me to connect with the coven but also to myself.

One by one, the women's eyes fluttered shut, and I closed mine, too. Elspeth began to speak again, this time in the language of her spells. Like before, I didn't quite comprehend the meaning, but it felt familiar, and I found myself joining in the chant, my mouth automatically forming the words, my tongue rolling over the complicated syllables. The sound was enchanting: eight women in perfect unison, in perfect synchronicity. I began to tremble. The women joined Elspeth now, echoing her words in a slow chant that rippled through the circle like a murmur.

I poured my concentration into the image of the hawk. But my mind had other ideas. I was suddenly transported back in time, and the image of the man in a brown robe appeared in my mind's eye. So much had happened lately, I'd almost forgotten that he'd appeared at my first magic circle. He hadn't spoken, simply given me a warm smile and a simple nod of the head as though we knew each other. Why was I thinking about him now when I had other pressing concerns? My eyes flicked open as if of their own accord.

And there he was.

In the middle of the circle, the ghostly outline of a man: tall, slender, but instead of the brown robe, he was wearing a pair of blue jeans and a white shirt. He looked much younger than I'd remembered in ordinary, modern clothing. His light brown hair was swept back, his skin tanned and smooth. But, as before, he was smiling at me. He felt so real, like I could reach out and touch him, but the flickering outline of his body left me in no doubt that this was a man who had passed over to the other side.

My eyes darted around the circle, but the other women were still engrossed in their chanting. No one else was seeing what I was seeing. And what was that exactly? Could this really be who I thought it was?

I opened my mouth, ready to let a hundred questions fire out, willing to reveal my gift of seeing the departed to the entire coven in exchange for some answers. But before I could let loose, the smile faded from his lips and he began to speak.

"Listen to me, Poppy. Listen carefully. You must leave this place. There are those who would do you harm."

He knew my name. He knew me. I shook my head. That

was not what I wanted to hear. No more cryptic warnings. I wanted answers. No more fooling around.

"Katie Donegal told me that my mother was pregnant when she worked in the kitchen. Is that true?"

His face softened. "You know it is."

I felt a tightness in my throat. I was nervous to voice aloud what I was certain was true. "And it was me she was carrying."

He nodded.

This was the final confirmation I'd been right. All my sleuthing had led to this moment. My eyes filled with tears. I let them run down my face. I looked to the old woman who'd called me Valerie the first time I came to Broomewode. She'd given me such a gift in that moment. The first clue to who I was.

I turned back to the man. "You know me."

He smiled sadly at me. "Poppy," he said gently, "I can't imagine you having any other name."

"Who are you?" I whispered, all my energy dissolving, waiting for him to say the words that I knew in my heart were true.

"My identity can only put you in more danger. Trust that you were created out of love and I only want to see you safe. Your quest is dangerous. Leave this place."

But I knew I wouldn't leave. I'd come too far. And I knew by his tone, by the way he was warning me in that gently chiding voice I'd been spoken to as a kid, that this was my birth father. I stifled my tears. Later I could cry all I wanted to, but now wasn't the time to get emotional. It was time for answers. His edges began to flicker, the softness of his outline slowly dissolving. Suddenly, I realized that while my mom appeared to me as a vision, this man, my birth dad, was a ghost, and that must mean he was dead. Before I could ever process that information, the edges around the man began to flicker with more urgency. He was going to disappear.

"Wait," I cried out. "Are you my father? What happened to you? Is my mother still alive?"

But he was gone.

I could have screamed. Surely if this was my dad, he owed me more than a warning. I wanted to understand what had happened. I needed facts, not vague warnings. I shook my head, and the tears cascaded down my cheeks. I wiped at them roughly with the fabric of my cardigan. I didn't want to cry. I had to be strong enough to keep searching for Valerie. And I certainly wasn't going to let his warning get in the way. After all, I had Team Poppy by my side, and if a girl couldn't keep safe with a coven of sisters, a magical amethyst necklace, a protection spell, a kitten, dog, hawk—and even a troublesome spirit like Gerry—well then, I didn't deserve my witchy stripes.

The chanting stopped, and one by one, the women opened their eyes.

No one had heard our conversation. There was so much to learn about how magic worked. I must've looked a real mess because, like a chain reaction, as we released hands, the women came closer, some hugging me, some offering a touch on the shoulder or a whisper of encouragement.

"Poppy dearest, what happened?" Elspeth asked.

I swallowed. It was hard to get used to speaking freely. All my life, I'd learned to keep quiet about my gift, to hide away what made me, well, unique. But now I had a safe space to be myself—ghosts and all.

I took a deep breath and explained that a ghost had appeared in the center of the circle.

"He was warning me to leave Broomewode," I told the women. "He said that I'm in danger."

Elspeth furrowed her brow. "It's not the first time you've received this kind of warning, Poppy. I'm starting to worry that the protection spell and the vigilance of me and your sisters isn't enough."

I could see where she was going and hastened to stop her. "Please don't tell me to leave. I can't. I won't."

"Let's combine our powers," Susan suggested. "What use is a coven if it can't protect our most vulnerable?"

"We can try," Elspeth said, but she still looked worried. She instructed everyone to join hands again. The electricity began to flow through me once more, and I gripped the women's hands tightly.

"Let us join together under the power of the full moon and supercharge our strength by speaking the protection spell as one."

The women nodded and smiled at me.

Earth, Fire, Water, all three,
Elements of Astral, I summon thee,
By the moon's light,
I call to thee to give us your might.
By the power of three
We conjure thee
To protect our innocent Poppy.
So we will, so mote it be.

There was no denying the ripple of power that coursed

through my hands that were linked with the other witches. The candles flickered, and a soft breeze blew through the stones and lifted my hair.

The calm I'd felt earlier returned, and I thanked the women, hugging each one with a force that I hoped conveyed my gratitude rather than feeling like they'd been mowed down by a bear.

Eve was last, and as I drew back, she suggested that when the others left, we join forces with Susan and Elspeth to cast a spell on the earl to ruin his aim. "Protection's all very well, but sometimes it helps to disarm the enemy."

I grinned. My kinda gal.

We said our goodbyes, the candles still burning brightly, and then took up position in the center of the stones.

"My dearest sisters," Eve said. "Since Poppy has brought it to our attention that Lord Frome is not respecting our wildlife, we must intervene and do what we can to preserve the natural world." A twinkle came into her eye. "And in this case, we may have to get a little mischievous. We'll put a protection spell on the wild birds of Somerset. If that causes the earl to lose his shooting aim as a consequence—well then, so mote it be."

She paused, and we joined hands.

"I'm most worried about the hawk that seems to hover near me," I reminded them.

Elspeth spoke. "The four of us represent each of the classical elements. I am air; Poppy, you are water; Eve is earth, and Susan is fire."

At this, Susan grinned, and for the first time, I made the connection with her fiery red hair. And her temperament, too. She was a passionate woman. Eve was so down to earth and homely that it made perfect sense she represented the earth, and Elspeth was so calm and all-knowing—like a perfect blue sky.

Elspeth began to chant in that ancient language, and although I didn't know what she was saying, I found that the words came to me again, like they'd been planted in my mouth. I closed my eyes and focused on the hawk, calling to mind its grand wingspan, then imagining it soaring free and undisturbed above the Broomewode hills.

When we finished, Elspeth drew us into a hug.

"Take that, Lord Frome," I whispered.

"Quite," said Elspeth in her delicate manner. "Take that!"

And then, out of the blue, a thought struck. Did the hawk have something to do with my dad?

CHAPTER 6

"Pops, you've really got to get a good night's sleep the night before filming."

Gina, my best friend and the show's makeup and hair artist, stood back as I accidentally yawned in her face while she was applying gloss to my lips. Oops.

"I'm sorry," I said while she tissued away the colored gloss she'd dabbed on my chin. But that was all I could say. How could I begin to explain to Gina what I'd gotten up to last night? It was wonderful having a bunch of new sisters, but it was widening the gap between me and my best friend. We'd always shared everything as kids, and when I moved back to England, we'd picked up where we left off. Gina knew all my embarrassing crushes, how bad my moves were on the dance floor, and she knew I wasn't exactly like other people. But now that I knew I was a witch, it was like I had a whole other life going on. It was making me uncomfortable.

"Honestly, these dark circles under your eyes could eclipse a full moon."

I snapped my eyes open. There was no way Gina could know about my goings-on with the moon, could she? Best friends did pick up vibes from each other. I decided to tell her that the moon was actually the reason I looked so tired.

"Did you know it was a full moon last night?" I asked. "I was restless, so I walked around the grounds after dinner. It was beautiful. The whole of the village looked shimmery in its light, like the surface of a rippling lake."

Gina squinted her eyes. "Never mind the poetry. You were meeting someone, weren't you?"

Again, I felt astonished at how perceptive she was. Had she seen the coven? Then I noticed the way she was looking at me. Not like I was a witch, but like I was a singleton who might like a partner someday. "No," I said, a little cranky. "I wasn't meeting a guy." As if I had time. "I'd tell you if there was anyone."

"There are some nice-looking guys on the crew. I wondered."

I shook my head. "I only have time for cakes."

"And the perfect winged eyeliner? What do you reckon? I'm going to do it in brown, not black, to suit your skin tone and personality. I don't want it to look like you're wearing a mask."

I smiled and closed my eyes. Gina was the queen of makeup. She always did what was best.

"You know, you did so well last week, Poppy, I really think you could win this thing."

I didn't want to go on camera with an eye injury, so I kept them closed, but I was surprised by Gina's statement.

"Are you serious?" I asked. "There's so much talent in the

group. Every week it gets tougher. I feel like I'm barely hanging on."

"All you've got to do is keep your focus. Which means no more late nights." She tapped me on the nose with a powder brush. "Open," she commanded. She appraised my finished look. "You look fabulous. I love that we did your hair like that."

I gently patted the bun Gina had defied gravity with, rolling my long, thick locks into the perfectly imperfect messy bun on the top of my head. She pulled a couple of dark strands away from my face and tucked them behind my ear. It was a great look to finish off the denim shirtdress Gina had picked out for me this week, which had pretty pearl buttons from neck to knee.

"Bellissima!" said Florence, walking towards us with her million-dollar smile.

Florence was, of course, already perfectly made up. She was wearing loose red trousers with a matching button-down shirt open at the neck to reveal an ornate gold locket at her throat. Her lips were the exact same shade of maroon as her outfit.

"Can't hold a torch to you, Florence," I said. Not for the first time, I thought about how Florence would end up cast in her own cooking show, or maybe a travel program with her talent for languages. She was beautiful, an accomplished actress, and she could cook. But it wasn't over yet. And was it my imagination, or was she a shade less friendly now that we were getting closer to the end of the competition?

Not that I could believe a woman like Florence would ever view me as competition. I was probably getting squirrelly from stress.

"Places, everyone," Fiona called out.

It was that time again. Soon the judges and the two comedians would stand at the front of the tent and announce our first challenge.

I went back to my workstation and gave myself a mental pep talk inspired by Gina's words of encouragement. *You've got this, Pops. You've practiced and prepared, and you know what you're doing. Just keep your eyes on the prize. It's within sight.*

Today, comedian Jilly took the lead and welcomed us back to the tent. Along with her signature blue glasses, she was wearing a typically lively combination of blue leopard-print trousers and a pale pink shirt, finished off with a hot pink lipstick. I loved how Jilly played with color and fashion —everything she wore was flamboyant but looked like it had been designed especially for her.

Jilly cleared her throat. "Bakers, the competition is as tough as the pancakes Arty made me for breakfast, and this week we're going to need you to put your best foot forward and really bring your A game to stay in the competition."

Thanks, Jilly, because so far we've been bringing our B game... And wait...was she joking, or had Arty really made her breakfast? I sneaked a glance at her fellow comedian, but his expression gave nothing away.

"And speaking of unusual couples," Arty said, "that's the theme for your first challenge of cake week. We'll begin with your signature bake, and Jonathon here will tell us a bit more of what our master bakers are looking for."

Jonathon smiled and stepped forward. "We're looking for light, airy sponges and rich, crumbly frangipanes, or perhaps a few of you are planning a chiffon cake. Pair two or more unusual ingredients and make them work together. And we want to be wowed. You'll have three and a half hours to complete your bake."

Arty gave the starting cue, and I took a breath, looking around to gain support from these bakers who'd become friends. There were fewer stations this week, which I knew meant my chances of going home were that much greater, but I liked how close we'd become as a group.

I smiled at Maggie and Gaurav. I was late to breakfast this morning and hadn't managed to catch up with the other contestants yet. I was looking forward to having chats over lunch. It also meant I didn't know what everyone else was planning today. It would be interesting to see everyone's bakes coming together as the morning progressed.

While I'd been musing, Elspeth wished us luck and Jilly called time.

I had to spring into action pronto to make sure my basil cream infusion had enough time to...well, infuse. There was no time to waste.

I poured the cream into a saucepan and, while it was coming to a simmer, bruised my larger basil leaves by hitting them repeatedly with the dull side of a knife, thinking of the earl aiming at the hawk as I did so. What a cathartic way to start my bake. I stirred them into the cream, removed the mix from the heat, and then covered the pan with plastic wrap and left it to steep.

Okay, Pops, all on track. Now for the sponges.

But of course, that's exactly when Arty decided to come and terrorize me with his questions. I fixed my face with a wide grin as he approached with cameras and steeled myself for being teased.

"Poppy, a little birdie told me that you're making a layer

cake," Arty said. "But I see that you've only got two cake tins greased up and ready to go here."

Thanks for counting to two for me, Arty.

"That's right. I'm making two deep sponges and then slicing them in half to make four layers."

You're not the only one who can count.

I tipped my flour, baking powder, baking soda and salt into a huge glass bowl and began whisking them together by hand, smiling at Arty as he asked me about my unusual flavor combination.

"It's not something we come across every day. I'm more of a basil pesto kinda guy myself. Basil and strawberries?"

I dutifully laughed. "Well then, I hope you'll be pleasantly surprised. Basil and strawberry work really well together." I gestured at the saucepan. "At home, once I've strained the basil leaves from the cream, I'd refrigerate the mix for at least five hours. But I don't have that long today. I figured *The Great British Baking Contest* fridges are superior to my old one in my cottage at home, so hopefully it'll chill faster here."

"You tell that fridge who's boss."

"I'm sure I could bend it to my will," I said with a wink. Whoa, where did flirty Poppy come from? All this time hanging out with Florence was clearly having an effect.

Arty laughed. "So the butter goes in next?" he inquired, peering into my bowl.

"Almost. I'll beat butter and sugar together next."

I tapped the side of the mixer, thankful it was the same brand as the one I had back home, and said as much to Arty. "Having to use equipment that isn't mine is one of the toughest parts of the show. Baking's a dance of sorts between you and your tools, and if you aren't used to your partner's particular movements, well, then, some toes might get trodden on."

I'd been doing this long enough that I was used to the rhythm of how the show worked. I'd become better at keeping my cool and staying on top of the recipe while chatting with the judges and comedians. I still felt as nervous and rattled on the inside but was better at hiding it.

Arty was about to reply when a great commotion erupted outside the tent. It sounded like chanting. Really loud chanting. I opened my mouth and then closed it again. Apart from the constant whirr of mixers and the odd shriek of joy or disappointment, the tent was usually a pretty quiet place. It had to be, for filming.

"What on earth?" Arty said, bemused.

"Cuuuuut!" Fiona yelled, and then quieter, but only a little, "What the bollocks is going on?" She really did say bollocks, which would have delighted me if I didn't know that filming was going to be delayed as a result of whatever was going on outside the tent. I was sneakily glad my basil would have more time to infuse, but if we were being delayed this early in the day, we could end up filming really late. And I was already tired from missing so much sleep last night.

I put down my spoon and joined the rest of the contestants and crew speeding over to the tent's entrance to see what on earth was happening.

Hamish was standing in the entrance staring out, and I tapped his shoulder.

"Look," he said, moving to one side and pointing.

Outside, a small group of determined-looking and very noisy people were marching across the lawn right in front of the tent. There were seven, maybe eight of them, men and women, and they were holding placards, but I couldn't quite make out what the slogans said. I recognized them, though, with their bucket hats and binoculars.

Fiona brushed past us and strode towards the group, who didn't bother to slow their march on her behalf.

"What are you doing?" Fiona said, forced to march at the same pace as the group. "Can't you read?" She gestured at the signs that sprung out from the grass: "Quiet Please Filming In Progress."

I'd never heard Fiona speak so sharply before. She must have been at her wits' end with the drama going on around here. How had the group managed to march past the security guards? I hadn't even been able to drop ingredients off yesterday without the Spanish Inquisition.

I stepped forward to get a better look. The lady talking to Fiona was Marlene, the woman I'd spoken with from the bird-watching group yesterday and seen again in Susan's pamphlet. If I'd thought she'd been abrupt and a little abrasive then, it was nothing compared with the shrill tone she was taking with Fiona now. Still striding, she said, "This is an ancient public rights of way, and no one can stop us traversing it." The woman's eyes flashed, and she turned her placard so the cameras could film it, as though this was the nightly news crew.

Her placard read: "Public Rights of Way for the PUBLIC."

Not the most memorable phrase, perhaps, but this group was doing their best to chant it with passion. Well, they were British, so it was a restrained passion.

Fiona looked like she wanted to take one of those placards and bang it over Marlene's head. "Actually, we can. All we've done is alter the course of the rights of way whilst we're

66

filming. It's temporary. There are many other routes around the grounds you can follow. But right now, time is money, and you can't delay the show for"—she waved an arm around —"whatever this is."

I squinted. "Save Our Wild Birds" had been painted in green across another of the placards.

The woman stopped pacing and stared Fiona in the eye. "I understand, but you see, the earl would like nothing more than to stop people coming onto his property. He does not like to share. Diverting the paths is one way he tries to take back ancient rights of way, and we must stop him."

Fiona's sigh of despair was audible even from where I was standing. "But we're filming *The Great British Baking Contest*. You must know this show brings wealth to the local economy and boosts tourism."

"Cakes are all very well and nice," Marlene argued. "I'm partial to a slice of lemon poppy seed myself, but they don't stand up to how important it is to protect the wild birds of England. And that is exactly what we are going to do."

Fiona was wringing her hands, nonplussed. But luckily the woman and her crew marched off in the direction of the manor house. *Good luck with that one, Benedict.*

Fiona marched over to where Donald Friesen, the series producer, was tearing into Martin, the new security guard. I would *not* want to be Martin right now.

"Ooch," Hamish exclaimed. "Who knew that twitchers could be so feisty?"

"Twitchers?!"

"Ach, I'm just being silly. That's the nickname for bird-watchers, especially the kind who like to spot as many birds as possible as quickly as possible."

"I think that lively group are more like environmental campaigners. Or at least their leader is. I met her yesterday. She's pretty fierce."

Hamish laughed. "So's Fiona. I was afraid I'd have to wrestle those two apart."

"Okay everyone," Fiona said, clapping her hands together like we were in school. "*That* particular show is over. Now let's get back to ours."

I rushed back to my batter and began creaming the butter and sugar. There wasn't a minute more to waste. But as I added the flour, my thoughts strayed. Could the sudden appearance of the Somerset Wild Bird Protection Society have something to do with the spell we cast last night? I'd put a lot of energy into visualizing the hawk, not to mention willing the earl to get his comeuppance. Elspeth had warned me that spells weren't always straightforward: When you asked for something, you could never be entirely sure how your request would be granted.

Had we caused these people to appear by putting a protection spell on the birds of Broomewode? Or was my sleuthing brain working overtime and it was merely a coincidence? Marlene was already irate when I met her yesterday. After the magic circle, I tried my best to avoid ruminating as to how my dad and the hawk were connected and tried to focus on getting a good night's sleep before filming began. But the question mark floating over the connection was bugging me.

I'd have to work to solve that particular mystery. Now it was time for whisking, not wondering. At least my mind could be at ease knowing that the Bird Society were already doing something to help protect the hawk.

For now, I had to concentrate on my signature bake. I picked up my carton of buttermilk and added it to the mix. Everything was riding on me keeping it together this weekend, and I wasn't about to let myself get distracted by trespassing twitchers.

CHAPTER 7

"You've half an hour to go, bakers," Arty called out. I tried not to let the panic set in. I'd been checking on my basil cream infusion every few minutes, but the mixture still wasn't set. Now I had no option but to admit it needed a burst in the blast chiller. I was going to have to watch it very carefully to make sure it didn't freeze. It was cake week, not ice-cream week, after all.

As I collected my bowl from the fridge, I could tell the other contestants were feeling the pressure, too. Calm and steady Daniel, the man used to reassuring people as he pulled their teeth or installed their braces, was now red, sweating profusely, and muttering so many obscenities under his breath that Fiona kept telling him to *cut it out.*

With my cream safely in the freezer and my sponges still cooling, I went to his workstation to see if there was anything I could say or do to ease his stress.

"It's all going wrong, Poppy," he said, looking forlorn.

And I could see why. Daniel had been attempting to create a chocolate and raspberry sponge, but the sides of his sponge were burned. Like me, he was making a layer cake, but with three larger sponges, rather than four slimmer layers. His sponges were huge, and I could see that he'd left them in the oven too long, afraid they'd not cook all the way through. Now it'd gone the other way.

He was furiously straining a raspberry coulis, taking his frustration out on a poor sieve. He wasn't exactly walking on the culinary wild side if he'd chosen chocolate and raspberry as his odd couple. Maybe there was cardamom or something in the mix. I didn't ask, as I didn't want to stress him further.

"It's not so bad," I said, turning the cooling rack round to examine them more carefully. "Just cut the burnt ends to make a slightly smaller cake," I suggested. "No one will be any the wiser."

"No one except the millions of viewers who just watched me burn a simple chocolate sponge..."

Hmm, good point.

"Don't worry," I replied. "It's about the taste and look of the final product."

Daniel took a deep breath and eased his grip on the sieve. "You're right, you're right. I'll cut them off. Hopefully the burned taste won't permeate the rest of the sponge."

I rubbed his back. "That's the spirit. You've got this. What's your filling?"

"Chocolate fudge ganache. And I'll drizzle the finished cake with raspberry coulis." He gave me a worried glance. "You don't think it's too strange? Chocolate with raspberry?"

"No. I really don't."

"Lovely," he said.

I was worried that the coulis might make the cake soggy. But now wasn't the time to make Daniel worry further. I flashed him a final encouraging smile and then went back to my workstation to macerate my strawberries and slice through my own sponges.

I took Susan's punnet of strawberries and chopped them into large chunks before scooping the lot into a bowl and showering them with sugar. Earlier, I'd tasted one of the fruits (a chef has got to know her own ingredients), and it was perfectly ripe and delicious—sweet too. So I decided not to use as much sugar as I'd been practicing with to make sure the tartness of the berry came through. I gave the mix a little stir so the sugar would dissolve evenly and put the bowl to one side. But I'd have to keep a close eye on them. I didn't want the berries to get too juicy and become soggy. Elspeth's biggest pet peeve was a cake with a "soggy bottom."

And as if I'd conjured her up with my thoughts, Elspeth approached my workstation, Jilly close behind. I steeled myself to talk through this tricky procedure. Despite my words of encouragement to Daniel, I felt suddenly shy and unsure of myself. But Elspeth's presence soon changed that, and as she came to stand by my side, I knew that I was in control and on schedule.

"Looks like you're about to embark on a little cake surgery," Jilly remarked, as I turned my now cool sponges onto a wooden chopping board.

"That's right. Move over, brain surgery—this little operation takes nerves of steel," I joked, and then made a silent wish that no real-life brain surgeons were watching.

I laid each cake flat and inhaled their buttery, vanilla scent. Delicious. "There truly is nothing like the smell of cake fresh out of the oven," I said. With a long, sharp knife, I bent down so that I was eye level with the sponge and then dragged the blade through its center to split the sponge in two.

I could have done without Jilly and Elspeth watching, and with them, of course, the camera, so I imagined millions of home viewers scrutinizing my every move. I held my breath as I sliced the sponges...but to my huge relief, I got through both cakes with no trouble.

"And voila, now we have four layers," I said to Elspeth. As though I hadn't been so shaky inside I was surprised the cake surfaces didn't look like corrugated cardboard.

It was hard to act like Elspeth was just a judge on the show to me. I kept wanting to hug her or waiting for her to hug me and tell me that I'd be fine. But Elspeth remained a consummate professional. Nothing in her demeanor gave any indication that she was actually my witchy godmother as well as cake critic.

"What's going to glue those puppies together?" Jilly asked.

Good question. My cream was still in the blast chiller. I really needed to run and check it wasn't forming icicles. I said as much to Jilly and Elspeth, explaining that because the infusion needed longer to emulsify than our allotted time, I'd left it in the blast chiller. I excused myself and, as gracefully as I could, sprinted to the other side of the tent.

I could feel the cameras trained on me—one behind, one to the side. I opened the door with my breath held.

The mix hadn't crystalized but set, as it should. I slid it out using oven gloves so that my hands wouldn't freeze and brought it back to my sponges. To my horror, Jilly and Elspeth hadn't moved on. They were waiting to see if my basil infusion would work. At least I could prove myself right at this stage.

Jilly leaned over my bowl. "It's an...interesting choice, to combine an herb most people associate with pizza with whipped cream." It sounded like she wouldn't be rushing in for a slice when the filming was done. "You've definitely got the odd couple brief."

Although I'd been expecting this kind of question, Jilly made it sound like I'd smashed up the rulebook. In fact, basil and strawberry was a pretty tried and tested combo. I'd wanted to pair two flavors that worked, after all.

"Well," I started, setting up my trusty electric mixer and then adding a little more sugar to my chilled bowl, "it's an intuitive combination." I paused for a second, trying to gather my thoughts. I needed to answer this question ASAP and get this cream whipped. "Strawberries can often be a hit or miss fruit. Sometimes they're too watery, sometimes too tart. But by combining them with basil, its subtle, almost clove-like notes actually enhance the berries' natural flavor. It becomes more rounded, more piquant."

Elspeth looked impressed by my answer, and I glowed.

"Lucky for me, these berries were picked at Broomewode Farm only yesterday, so they haven't traveled and they're grown in rich, well-kept soil. And the same is true of the basil I'm using. Mixed together, these ingredients should elevate each other." I only hoped I'd judged the sugar and water content of the berries right.

Elspeth nodded her head appreciatively, but Jilly still looked skeptical.

"I'm simultaneously excited and apprehensive about this, Poppy," Jilly said.

"Well, Jilly," I replied with as gracious a smile as I could muster at this point, "the proof will be in the pudding, as they say."

I excused myself to switch on my mixer, and my audience of two divided and went to speak to the other bakers. *Not a moment too soon.*

I turned the dial to a high setting and whisked the cream infusion. I needed to wait until soft peaks formed, but if they began to stiffen, it would be game over. I stared into the depths of the bowl as if it was an oracle and I was waiting to receive instructions. I stopped and tasted the mix. It was delicious but a little subtle. I added a handful of small torn basil leaves and let the whisk break them into pretty green flecks.

Over the whirr of the mixer, I could hear Florence chatting to Elspeth. I'd been so absorbed in what I was doing that I hadn't even asked Florence what her plan was. Last week, she'd been at the top and then near the bottom of the competition. Now I could see that she was perfectly relaxed as she gestured to her sponge.

"It's all about the balance of the flavors with this one," Florence said confidently, flashing her perfect white teeth. She didn't look stressed in the slightest. Not a bead of sweat or even a slight furrow of the brow. How did she do it? "It's a twist on an Italian specialty. My sponge is soaked in Cinzano and strong coffee, and I'll pair it with lemon custard." She was using candied lemon slices and coffee beans in her decoration.

"If I got soaked in Cinzano, I'd need strong coffee too," Jilly said and deadpanned to the camera.

It took Florence a second to get the joke, then she laughed, the sound as gorgeous as the rest of her.

Perfect peaks achieved, I turned off my mixer. The next

step was to fold in the macerating strawberries. First I had to strain the fruits, capturing the juice in a measuring jug so that I could drizzle it over the finished layer cake later. As I stirred, I continued to eavesdrop on Florence.

Florence said, "I'll flavor the custard with limoncello. When I summer by the lakes, I find it's the tastiest way to end a lunch or dinner. Sometimes even breakfast." She chuckled.

"I can't say I've ever indulged in it myself," Jilly said.

"Oh, you simply must try it," Florence cooed. "It's an Italian lemon liqueur, mainly produced in Southern Italy. You sip it in small glasses as a digestif. But for today's bake, I've made my own in advance. It's a family recipe, combining vodka, sugar and the best unwaxed lemons from the Amalfi Coast that I could find."

"A right little mixologist we've got here," Jilly said, obviously impressed. Weren't the comedians supposed to stay neutral on the show? Florence was getting a far better reaction than I had. I tried not to worry and instead concentrated on sandwiching my cakes together with the cream infusion.

But now I couldn't help but tune in to Florence's voice. "And," she continued, "the citrus of the lemon really brings out the zesty notes of the basil."

My head snapped up. Oh no! Florence was using basil as a key ingredient, too? How had I not found this out sooner? Now it was like we were head to head in the competition. And I didn't fancy my chances against Florence. She was describing how she'd made a special limoncello glaze and was now putting the final touches to sugared freeze-dried basil leaves that went in some complicated pattern with the coffee beans and lemon slices.

All those extra details and bold flavor combinations were

going to add up to something truly special. I tried to stop my heart from sinking.

I sandwiched my final layer of sponge and cream and set about coating the top with luscious peaks of cream and a careful pile of berries.

"Five minutes, bakers," Arty called out.

Great, just enough time to slice those figs to decorate the base.

But from the sounds of it, not everyone was on track. I looked up. Amara was flapping around her workstation, cries of "I'm not finished, I'm not finished" echoing around the tent. Even Maggie, usually the serene one during filming and utterly absorbed in her bake, looked stressed. I tried to focus my energy to send them both good vibes across the tent. It was so hard watching the other bakers struggle. I knew exactly the kind of panic they were experiencing. And today the hours had really flown by. Before I knew it, I was placing the final strawberry slices on the top of my cake when Arty called out that our time was up.

I stood back from my workstation, a little amazed at what I'd managed to produce. The cake was tall and beautiful, the cream oozed gently at the sides without slipping down, and the berries were plump and bright, perfectly set off by the sliced figs around the base. What a good idea from Susan. I'd have to find some way to thank her.

"Please bring your cakes to the table, bakers," Elspeth commanded.

And here we were again, a solemn line of exhausted bakers, nervously carrying our wares to be judged.

Set out at intervals on the table, the cakes looked delightful. A bright array of colors and styles. It was funny—now that we were on week five of the competition, I felt like I could tell which cake belonged to which contestant. Maggie had kept to her traditional roots and made a beautiful stacked Victoria sponge cake. It looked like a wedding cake, decorated with flowers, fruits and nuts. I wondered if Maggie had believed mixing her decorations would fit the bill?

Gaurav had gone with an upside-down cake, but he'd combined pineapple with coconut and caramelized rhubarb. It was pretty but not his best.

But then I saw Florence's cake. In a flash, my confidence crumbled and imposter syndrome took over. I couldn't help but compare my cake to her creation. It looked so special—authentic while being innovative.

Who was I even trying to kid? I thought I'd really outdone myself by using basil, but it wasn't original. What if I hadn't done enough? My stomach went cold, and I had my usual flashbacks to sitting at the back of a math class, worrying that I'd be called on to come up to the board and complete an equation. When our cakes were being judged, while we sat there pretending we didn't know cameras were recording our every emotion, it was like our souls were bared.

"This is a very impressive array of cakes," Elspeth said, smiling generously and taking time to look each baker in the eye. "I can see how much you're all improving. This is going to be a tricky one to judge."

Time slowed as I watched Jonathon and Elspeth slice into each cake.

"Lovely presentation," Jonathon said when they started with Maggie's.

"Is it a bit ordinary?" Elspeth asked. I glanced at Maggie, but she had a sly look, almost as though she were secretly amused. Then Jonathon cut into the cake and everyone said, "Aah." The contestants as well as the judges.

Her cake was an array of gorgeous stripes. "But how did you do it?" Jonathon asked as though he'd never seen colored cake before.

"I used beet for that magenta color, pistachio for the soft green, spinach for the darker green and blueberry for the blue."

"Gorgeous," Elspeth said. "And the taste?"

She and Jonathon both took a forkful. As he often did, Jonathon waited for Elspeth to give her opinion first. She nodded. "Amazing. Beautiful flavor, very nice crumb, and the décor is exquisite. Well done."

Maggie beamed as they moved on. As usual, they doled a mix of compliments and criticisms—the expressions of the other bakers matching their rising and falling hopes. Hamish had perhaps the most interesting combination. He'd used the Scottish thistle. "I foraged for them myself. Very carefully. Using gloves," he told Jonathon when he asked. "Also dark beer and some dry mustard."

"Interesting," said Jonathon on first tasting the chocolate cake.

"Indeed. Very piquant. But a little heavy," Elspeth said.

Gaurav received praise for his tropical creation and Daniel criticism for the burned edges he hadn't quite managed to disguise. "I think your flavor combination could have been more daring," Elspeth finished.

Amara seemed to neither excite nor disappoint the judges, and then there were two left. Two basil cakes. On the surface, they were nothing alike, but their flavor profile was two sides of the same coin—like twin sisters separated at birth.

Elspeth complimented the neat layers of my cake and its bright colors. "But does it taste as good as it looks?" she asked. Jonathon nodded solemnly, and I tried to control my face as he picked up the knife and cut through the cream.

Jonathon spoke first. "This is rather tasty. The fruit is sweet and sticky, the cream rich and gooey, the sponge is fluffy. Only thing is—I'm not getting enough of the basil flavor."

"Indeed," Elspeth said, nodding. "So much to like here. It's a well put together cake. But that basil flavor is lacking. I think perhaps the cream needed to infuse for longer."

I hung my head. *Lack of flavor.* I felt like such a dummy. I knew it had been a gamble trying to squeeze in making that basil cream. And now my cake had underwhelmed the judges. How could I make such a rookie mistake? But there was no time to ruminate as the judges bit into Florence's cake.

"Bellissimo!" Jonathon said. "I feel as if I've been transported to the Amalfi Coast. I'm getting fresh, zesty lemon, green, herby basil, and it all goes so well with the coffee custard."

"Mmm," Elspeth agreed. "This is really quite something. A flavor explosion, I'd say."

If my head could have sunk to my knees, it would have. *A flavor explosion.*

Florence had delivered. My pretty layer cake was the frustrated bridesmaid to her glorious bride.

Elspeth and Jonathon moved to the back of the tent to confer, and I looked at the other contestants to gauge how they were feeling. Not a single confident face—except

Florence. She was glowing with pride. And deservedly so. I just wished that I didn't feel like I was the ugly twin sister.

Elspeth and Jonathon returned, and the cameras changed angles to capture our reactions. I tried not to look as downhearted as I felt.

"Bakers," Elspeth began, "this was a fun round of signature bakes, and we appreciate your clever use of ingredients. But Jonathon and I are in agreement that by far the most impressive cake was..."

If only I could have a thousand dollars to correctly guess the winner.

"...Florence!" Jonathon finished.

Well duh, I wanted to say. Instead, I clapped her on the back and said congratulations.

"In second place is Maggie," Jonathon continued.

"And in third place we have...Poppy."

"What?!" I accidentally cried out, incredulous. "I thought I'd blown it."

Jonathon shook his head, laughing. "Not at all. It was a delightful cake which demonstrated your flair for baking. Just a little more basil next time."

The cameras stopped rolling, and I let out my breath.

I was so relieved. And famished! Thank goodness it was time for lunch.

CHAPTER 8

*E*n masse, we moved to the buffet table that had been erected outside the tent as we'd baked. Today we had a greater variety than usual, and it was hard not to drool at the array of food on offer. Sausage rolls, mini quiche Lorraines, mini tandoori chicken kebabs on sticks, a green tomato salad with vinaigrette, and a creamy-looking potato salad topped with chives. Yum.

"Wow, they really went the whole hog with today's spread," Daniel said, reaching for a plate. "What do you think this means? The show's been canceled and we're all going home?"

I managed to smile, but I couldn't really deal with his gallows humor. Too much was in the balance for me to even contemplate that this could be my last weekend.

"Don't tempt fate," I said. "She's a cruel mistress. One foul word and she might change the course of your destiny."

"Didn't have you down for that earth-mother stuff," he joked back.

Well, actually, Daniel, my element is water, not earth, so in a way you're right.

I picked up a plate and began helping myself to salads and a couple of chicken kebabs. I was going to have to keep my strength up for the technical bake this afternoon, after all.

The contestants had made a picnic area of sorts, and I was about to join them when I heard a familiar woof. And I do mean *familiar.*

"Sly?" I said, turning around.

The border collie came bounding over, but straightaway, I noticed that there was no ball in his mouth.

I set my plate back on the table. "What are you doing here, boy?" I asked, bending down to give him a stroke. "Is something wrong?" I thought Sly was trying to communicate something with his presence. "Is Susan okay?" I asked him. He barked happily. "Okay, so it's not that," I mused. Was I being paranoid? Sly did like to venture away from the farm and go off on his own expeditions. Maybe he was hoping for a slice of cake or more likely a piece of chicken from my plate.

"Don't tell anyone," I whispered, setting down a chunk of meat. He gobbled it up. But I wasn't convinced that Sly was only here to mooch.

Instead of sitting with the others, I took my plate and walked away from the tent in the direction of the manor house. Sly ambled along at my side.

The grass had been freshly mown, and its clean scent reset my nose after hours of smelling nothing but cake. The day was warm, and apart from a few white cotton wool clouds, the sky was clear blue. I checked for the hawk. Nothing. I hoped he was okay. A single green leaf fluttered by on the breeze, dropped into the lake, and floated silently on the surface. Was that why Sly was here? Was he guiding me to the lake?

Before I could get any closer, a superior-sounding voice blasted through the air.

"Ms. Applebaum, that is really *none* of your concern."

Ms. Applebaum? The voice was coming from the direction of the staff entrance. I circled the lake until a group of people came into view. It was the bird-watchers...and the earl! Aha, good for them. They'd cornered Lord Frome and from the looks of it were giving him a real earful about his hunting antics.

Ever the loyal sidekick, the gamekeeper, Arthur, stood slightly in front of his boss like a human shield. What did Arthur think these bird-watchers were going to do? Take down the earl with their binoculars? Marlene was at the front, wagging her finger in Arthur's face. Her last name must be Applebaum. She looked as stern as a schoolteacher. Maybe the earl had finally met his haughty match. I looked down to say as much to Sly, but he'd disappeared. Was this what he'd wanted to show me?

I felt eyes on my back and turned to see Edward regarding the scene with mirth. He had a pair of gardening shears in one hand and raised the other in hello. I smiled, and he gestured for me to join him.

"It's always nice to see your boss get taken down a peg or two by a pensioner," Edward said, laughing. His pale skin had turned pink in the sun, and he slipped a green baseball cap over his blond hair.

"I suspect Marlene over there isn't afraid of anyone. Not even the great Lord Frome. She cares more about wildlife than titles. And I don't think she's going to back down before she gets him to change his ways."

"Lord Frome gives as good as he gets. And he doesn't take kindly to those who differ from his way of thinking." He lowered his voice. "Especially the peasants."

I chuckled and looked again at the scene. Even though he was greatly outnumbered, the earl didn't seem in the slightest bit disturbed by being faced with a rowdy group of birdwatchers. He seemed annoyed by the inconvenience. The earl argued loudly with Marlene, and I was surprised by his lack of decorum. Wasn't he supposed to represent the British aristocracy? Where was his stiff upper lip?

"How's it going in the tent?" Edward asked.

But before I could answer, Hamish's loud baritone voice called my name.

"Oops. Lunch break must be over," I said, excusing myself. It was time to put my head back in the baking game. But not before I scoffed the last of my potato salad, of course.

CHAPTER 9

"Where did you disappear off to?" Florence asked as we stood at our workstations waiting for the technical challenge to be announced.

What could I reply? My coven sister's familiar arrived and led me to a group of angry bird-watchers?

"I needed some fresh air. I went for a walk. Hamish had to come and find me," I said sheepishly.

Florence raised a groomed brow. "After standing up for hours slaving over an electric mixer, I should have thought a nice sit-down would be in order." She waved a wooden spoon in my direction. "I've spent enough weekends with you to know that when you suddenly disappear into thin air, bad things happen. You need to be more careful."

I gulped. It was unlike Florence to be so serious. I was touched that she didn't want me to mess this up. I *was* her competition, after all.

"You're right. I'm back, refreshed. Bring on the next cake."

Florence chuckled. "That's more like it. Now, try hard but not too hard: I want to win this thing."

Don't we all, hon, don't we all.

Robbie came over to fix a glitch with my microphone.

"Thanks, Robbie," I said. "Sometimes I forget this thing is on me—which we were warned about right at the beginning of the contest."

"Right." He leaned in. "No snide remarks—we hear it all."

I cringed. Oh man, had I been muttering to myself when I was baking earlier? I did it all the time in my own kitchen, especially when Gateau was around and I could pretend I was talking to her. I tried to remember if I'd said anything unkind about another baker but didn't think I had. I'd probably just talked myself through the steps. Embarrassing but not mean.

Robbie grinned. "All done."

I thanked him and took a swig from my water bottle before the cameras rolled again. Gina rushed over to touch up my makeup.

"Why are you always late back to the tent, huh?" she asked, sweeping gloss across my lips.

I shook my head. "Long story."

"It always is with you." She gave my nose and forehead a quick powder and tucked a few strands of hair back into my bun. "You'll do," she said with a smile. "Keep up the good work, and don't let yourself get distracted. You've got that look in your eye."

"What look?"

"That quizzical putting-the-world-to-rights look you get. Whatever it is, keep your head in the game."

I nodded, remembering that everything I said was now on record, and turned my attention to reorganizing my utensils. One more bake for today and then I would go and find out what the Somerset wild bird people had said to the earl at lunchtime. I hoped they'd made it clear to him that hawks would be protected.

Arty took center stage and announced that today's challenge was one of Jonathon's all-time favorite cakes. I felt like groaning. Why did they always do this to us? Was there any cake that wasn't Elspeth and Jonathon's All-Time Favorite?

"Now this may come as a surprise to some of you, but Jonathon has got a bit of a sweet tooth, and he is a sucker for the American classic."

I felt my eyes widen. Please let it be––

"...known as angel food cake."

"Oh, no!" Amara cried across the room. "What's that?"

Elspeth nodded at Jonathon in that mom-like way she sometimes handled him with, and Jonathon cleared his throat. "Well, angel food cake is different from other sponge cakes because it contains no egg yolks or butter."

"What's the point, then?" Arty interrupted, and a few people laughed.

"The point is that the sponge is light as a cloud...so light, in fact, that it can float on a cloud so the angels can devour it. We can't let the devils have all the fun with their heavy devilish chocolate cake."

I couldn't help it—a smile spread across my face. Angel food cake was something I used to make with my mom back when we lived in Seattle. We had our own recipe, which was light and fluffy. We ate it with a raspberry sauce, not unlike the one Daniel made for his chocolate cake earlier.

"And we'll be asking you to make a passion-fruit curd to crown your angel food cakes."

Mmm. Delicious.

We were given pared-down recipes with basic ingredients we needed to include and told that we'd have two and a half hours to complete this challenge.

I set about getting my ingredients in order. From the afternoons I'd spent with Mom in the kitchen, I knew that the key to a good angel food cake was getting the egg whites whipped to the perfect meringue-like consistency. This took patience and diligence. A lot of it was judging by eye rather than following a strict recipe. I wondered how the perfectionists among us (me *so* not included) would deal with this.

While I'd been busy musing, Jonathon and Arty had arrived at my workstation. Great. I knew they'd come to the American first. But I was ready to wow them with my historical food knowledge.

"So, Poppy," Arty began, "I imagine you've had a few angel food cakes in your time."

"My mom used to make these when I was small," I said, weighing out my flour. "Sometimes, she liked to whip the egg whites by hand, rather than use an electric mixer, so that she could get more of a feel for the peaks."

"Are you about to go all food historian on us, Poppy?" Arty asked.

I smiled. "In fact, I do know that one of the first examples of an angel food cake appeared in *The Kentucky Housewife* in the eighteen hundreds."

"I think you know more than me, Poppy." Jonathon laughed, his blue eyes twinkling.

I giggled. As if I knew more about baking than the great Jonathon Pine. Even if he did have to rehearse his lines.

With my flour sifted and sugar added, I set my bowl aside. It was time to get on with those egg whites. Jonathon and

Arty moved on to Hamish, who was still studying the recipe and trying to work out whether to grease the ten-inch tube pan we'd been given. It had a cone-shaped kind of chimney in the center—like a Bundt pan but taller—and I could see that Hamish had never come across one before. My heart went out to him. I stopped separating my yolks and whites. "Don't grease it," I called out. "If you do, the batter can't cling to the surface of the pan and won't rise as high as it needs to."

"You lifesaver," Hamish said, his face softening as the panic left his body.

I smiled. I wasn't very good at this whole *I'm in competition with everyone* thing. But I couldn't watch poor Hamish flounder. I didn't want him to make a mistake before he'd even started. If he'd greased that pan, the cake wouldn't bake evenly, and the center would be raw when the outside edges were done. And no one wanted *that*.

I set to whisking the egg whites, watching until they became frothy, and then added lemon zest, lemon juice, cream of tartar, and a pinch of salt before whisking until soft peaks formed. But as I stared into the mix, I found my focus drifting. Where was the hawk? Was he safe? Why, in fact, did I assume the hawk was a he? I shook my head at my own assumptions.

I raised my head and looked out of the tent and into the sky. Patches of blue sky and a few puffy clouds, which, now that I thought about it, looked a lot like my egg whites. No hawk. *Focus, Pops. This bit is crucial.*

I increased the speed and added the remaining sugar one tablespoon at a time to form firm but not stiff peaks. Next, I sprinkled one-third of the flour mixture into the bowl and folded it in very gently. This was a delicate process. If I was too heavy-handed, then the batter wouldn't be light enough and would fail to rise. I kept going with the rest of the flour, making sure to keep as much air in the mix as humanly possible.

Whew, the last bit of flour had disappeared into the batter. Now it was time to transfer it to the angel food cake pan—another delicate procedure. No butterfingers need apply.

I lifted my head and surveyed the room. The atmosphere had changed, the way it often did during the technical challenge. Our signature bakes were about our personalities and recipes that had been tried and tested, some that had been handed down through the generations. But with the technical challenge, there was little room for our personalities to shine through. It was about precision, technique, and less about intuition. And it was the reason why everyone was looking so stressed. Including the unflappable Florence, and Maggie, the kindly grandma, whose stern expressions of concentration would have made me laugh if I hadn't known mine was exactly the same.

I gently ran a knife through the center of the batter to remove any pockets of air and then delivered the cake to the oven, wishing it well, and left it to cook for the next forty-five or so minutes. I took a moment and looked out into the skies again, closing my eyes for a second to channel my energy towards the hawk. My body began to fizz with electricity. I'd have to be careful not to short-circuit the ovens!

"Everyone should take a leaf out of Poppy's book," Arty said, bursting my energy surge. "She's so confident, she's having a quick standing kip."

I opened my eyes and felt my cheeks flame.

"Just gathering my thoughts before making the passion-fruit curd," I said sheepishly, hurrying back to my work-station.

And nearly jumped. Gerry was bent over in front of my oven. I'd all but walked through him. "Are you keeping a proper eye on this, Pops?" the world's most annoying ghost asked.

Reminding myself that everything I said could be heard by the sound techs, I kept going, feeling the cold as I walked through Gerry.

"Hey, watch it!" he said, turning to me in outrage. "It's different for the others. They can't help walking through me, but you did it deliberately."

I made eyes at him and a shooing motion with my hand when I thought no one was looking.

Gerry looked deeply hurt. "I'm only trying to help, and based on that pasty white mess in the oven, you need all the help you can get," he said. "Besides, I was bored."

"Go away," I mouthed the words.

He floated up to sit on top of my oven and pout. Just what I needed. A ghost with hurt feelings.

I turned to my workstation, but before I could start on the passion fruit, another commotion erupted outside the tent. And by now I knew exactly whose loud voice that was: Marlene Applebaum.

Once again, Fiona yelled, "Cut!"

Filming stopped. The crew and the rest of the cast all looked furious. But not as mad as Fiona. Even as she stomped toward the troublemaking bird-watcher, I was kind of impressed by Marlene's audacity. She and her colleagues were on a mission to teach the earl a lesson, and they were going to see it through to the bitter end. Of course they didn't care about a baking contest; they cared about protecting nature. I couldn't get mad about that. But I could get curious.

I joined the others crowded around the entrance to the tent. From the looks of it, all of us bakers were relieved to have a moment's respite from baking. The pressure was getting to us. But to my surprise, the source of the noise was twofold. Marlene was arguing with Martin, the security guard, who was trying to walk her and her group away from the tent.

"We're leaving, young man," Marlene said, drawing herself up to her full height. "No need to be rude."

"But you're causing a racket again. How many times must I remind you that the public throughway has been rerouted?"

"I could be your grandmother. Surely you could find it within yourself to talk to me with a little more respect," Marlene shot back, completely ignoring Martin's comment.

"Right," Fiona said, brushing past me. The bird-watchers stomped off so Fiona had no one to vent her wrath on but the security guard.

She approached Martin, who visibly shrank as he clocked the impending lecture coming his way.

"I don't know what's more frustrating," she began, "that I have to keep repeating myself or that my security continues to fail in his one objective—to keep the grounds quiet during filming."

"But—"

"You yelling at that crazy old woman isn't helping."

"Ooh, burn," Florence whispered.

Suddenly, Marlene turned back. Instead of continuing her tirade, she said, "It wasn't the lad's fault."

Fiona looked skyward and blew out a breath. "I know why you're here, and I appreciate your position, but we can't afford to have filming interrupted. It's a tight schedule and a tight budget, and there's no room for error."

Marlene looked somewhat abashed. "All right. We're leaving now. Along the ancient rights of way." She motioned to the group, who rallied round her, and then she led them away from the tent. I watched with a smile as she walked along the old rights of way triumphantly, her placard held up like a winning trophy.

Florence let out a short whistle. "I've got to say, I love that woman's sass. I hope I grow up to be like her—with better outfits, of course."

I laughed. "Marlene is pretty cool."

Florence raised a brow. "Honestly, how *do* you know everyone's name around here?"

"Let's just say I'm professionally nosy," I replied. "Let's get back to our bakes."

Florence linked her arm in mine, and we parted at our adjacent workstations.

When the cameras started rolling again, Jilly promptly began rapid-fire questions, and I could hear Hamish's voice boom across the tent as he explained his process. It tickled me how he still thought he had to speak louder when the cameras were on him.

Jonathon and Arty approached Florence. Good.

I tuned them out and tried to turn my concentration back to baking.

I mixed the ingredients for the curd together in a large pan and let it cook over a low heat, stirring every so often with a wooden spoon. It smelled incredible—zesty and fruity and sweet. It was a perfect accompaniment to the cake. Five minutes later, with the mixture now glossy and thick enough to coat the back of my spoon, I took it off the heat, spooned in the butter and then sieved the whole lot.

Phew. I was on a mission of my own.

Next up: the cream topping.

"Poppy! The cake," came an agitated voice.

I nearly strangled myself with my cry of panic.

I rushed over to the ovens, where Gerry was jumping up and down. "Thank you," I mouthed to him as I bent to peek through the window. Thankfully it had risen to great heights and had a pale golden appearance. Perfect.

Once the camera operator had filmed me taking my cake out of the oven, I speared the sponge with a skewer—it was clean—and then took the cake back to my workstation just in the nick of time.

Get it together, Pops. No time for a foggy brain.

I didn't even get mad when Gerry draped himself over my workstation, reminding me that he'd saved my butt. He had, but I'd thank him later.

To make sure that the cake didn't sink, it needed to cool upside down on a wire rack. I carefully turned it out and wished it well while it was cooling. At this point, every little bit helped.

Now I could start on the cream topping. I mixed in a teaspoon of vanilla essence and switched my trusty electric whisk on. I kept my head down and tried to ignore Gerry, plus keep my thoughts from straying back onto the whereabouts of the hawk or from wondering if our protection spell last night had accidentally called the bird-watchers onto the grounds. They were seriously stubborn. Was that natural or magic-made? I was desperate to ask Elspeth what she thought, but not with the cameras rolling.

I went through the rest of the recipe on autopilot, and before long, my sponge had cooled and I was smoothing the cream topping across its fluffy top. With less than five minutes to go, I cut a couple of fresh passion fruits in half, scooped out the seeds, and drizzled them over my cake. With a few seconds to spare, I was done when Arty called out, "Time's up, bakers. Put your equipment down and bring your cakes to the judging table."

I looked down at my cake, pleased with the results. Despite my wandering thoughts, I'd managed to keep on top of each step and finish in the allotted time. And for once, Gerry had done me a solid.

I picked up the plate and walked with the others back to the dreaded judging table. And then I got a shock. I must have had my head down during this challenge because I wasn't prepared for the variety of cakes in front of me. Had we not gotten the memo that this was the technical bake? We'd followed the same recipe and had the same utensils, but several of the cakes were so far from angel food cakes, it was like the devil himself had made them. Some had sunk. One had huge cracks the cream couldn't cover. Another hadn't cooled enough, and the cream topping was sliding down its sides. And by their faces, I knew that these struggling cakes belonged to Amara, Maggie, and Daniel, whose frowns and woeful expressions were being cruelly captured by the cameras. Again, I was surprised that Amara and Maggie had trouble with the recipe. It was simple enough, but you did need to know a few tricks to keep the batter light and airy. I felt for all of them and was almost ashamed of my insider knowledge as an American. For now, mine looked perfect—but would it taste the same way?

I braced myself as Jonathon and Elspeth commented on the look of each cake and then began the taste test. I winced as they sliced through each one, listening to their critiques of cakes that weren't airy enough or were downright dense; passion fruit that was overly sweet; cream that hadn't been whisked to stiff enough peaks. It was enough to make a girl cry—and they hadn't even gotten to my cake yet.

Finally, it was time to put me out of my misery. I held my breath as Elspeth delivered her verdict. She swallowed a mouthful of cake, but instead of a smile, her face became blank—almost as if she'd instructed her true reaction to disappear. Had she magicked away a grimace?

"It's a beautiful-looking cake," Elspeth began. "There's no denying it. But unfortunately, I think Poppy may have made a mistake with her measurements."

I gasped. What? Surely I hadn't been careless? The cake had risen perfectly. What could I have missed?

As if she could read my frantic thoughts, Elspeth quickly said, "I know this recipe inside out, and I'm certain it only has half the sugar it calls for. It's simply not sweet enough."

"Agreed," Jonathon said simply. "What a shame. The curd is superb, however."

My heart sank into my sneakers.

"That's very true," Elspeth said. "The passion-fruit curd goes some way to remedying the balance. It's fruity and sweet in equal measures. But it should be an accompaniment to the cake, not a necessity."

Ooof. I felt as if the earl had shot a few rounds right into my belly. *What an idiot, Pops. How could you have made such a silly mistake?*

Before I could properly gather my thoughts, Jonathon announced that they'd come to a decision.

"There was a clear winner in the technical challenge today. She's having an absolute blinder of a weekend. Congratulations Florence!"

I congratulated Florence, who swelled with pride, glowing and murmuring her thanks to everyone. She seemed genuinely taken aback to have won two challenges in one day. As I'd suspected, Maggie, Daniel and Amara took bottom places, Hamish was second, Gaurav third, and then there was me: in the middle of the pack.

This is not good enough, Poppy Wilkinson. I silently vowed to myself that tonight I'd rest up and get ready to give tomorrow's showstopper everything I had. No more distractions over the hawk. If I was voted out this week, then every clue I'd managed to piece together about my birth family would be for nothing. And I wasn't about to let that happen. No way.

CHAPTER 10

The pub was packed with groups starting their Saturday night early. I envied their carefree attitudes. They were mid-weekend—had spent the day doing whatever pleased them and still had the whole of Sunday to nurse any sore heads, take long walks across the beautiful Somerset Hills, or indulge in a roast lunch with all the trimmings. What I'd give to forget my responsibilities for a day and drive into town with Gina for a girls' night out.

Florence jabbed me in the ribs, breaking my feeling-sorry-for-myself moment.

"Do you think we'll even get a table?" she asked. "It's packed."

"You would have thought they'd reserve one for the contestants," Maggie added. "I so desperately need to sit down after so long on my feet."

"You're right," Gaurav said. "I'm going to find us a spot."

I linked arms with Maggie, and we walked to the bar, where there was a spare stool. Eve mouthed that she'd be with us in a minute.

I looked around the pub to see who'd taken our usual table and was surprised to see Marlene and her fellow bird-watchers having tea and coffee, wearing padded vests, and with binoculars hanging from the backs of chairs. They looked more relaxed than when they'd been marching past the tent but were deep in conversation. I was struck again by the thought that the magic circle had brought them back to Broomewode Village today. Had I also managed to spirit them to where I was staying?

"Darius is off tonight. If he was here, we'd have a table by now," Florence said in a smug tone.

"You know his work schedule?" I was surprised. Darius was gorgeous, but Florence didn't strike me as a woman who'd settle for a server, however hot he was.

As though she'd read my mind, Florence said in a low voice, "He's a fun distraction, darling. You run off to do whatever you do, and I have Darius."

I turned to Maggie, who'd settled on a stool. She checked her phone and then had to share the photos of her youngest grandchild starting to walk. I listened politely, with half my attention on the bird-watchers until curiosity began to eat away at me. I wanted to know if they'd managed to convince the earl to stop his shooting.

I hesitated, knowing that really I should keep out of any Broomewode politics until I'd baked a killer showstopper tomorrow, but what if I didn't get another chance to speak to the bird-watchers?

I told Maggie and Florence I'd be right back and then went to speak to Marlene.

She was mid-sentence but seemed to sense I was behind her and turned, her precise gray bob following suit. "Oh, hello," she said. "I met you yesterday. You're one of the bakers."

I nodded. "Yes. I'm Poppy." I glanced around and said softly, "I read a little about your society afterwards at Susan Bentley's farm."

Marlene nodded in what I could only guess was some kind of approval. "Susan is a good woman. She understands the natural order of the land."

I smiled. That was a nice way to put it.

"And we're very sorry for interrupting the show today," she continued. "It was nothing personal. But if people don't keep using the rights of way, the landowners will find excuses to close them to the public. The earl is determined to keep us off his property."

"I understand, I think. I'm afraid I don't know very much about rights of way. We don't have anything like it in the States."

At this admission, Marlene's eyes lit up. I'd obviously touched on one of her favorite subjects. She explained that ancient rights of way were old footpaths or bridleways across mountains, moors, heaths, downs, common land and some land around the England Coast Path. "People have walked these same paths for centuries. No matter that the land is privately owned. If we don't exercise our rights to cross the earl's lands, he'll try to take them back. He's a bad man."

"We follow the countryside code at all times," an older gentleman sitting beside her said. "The Society takes our responsibility towards the countryside very seriously. But time is ticking for our historic rights of way. Any pre-1949 footpaths, bridleways or byways that are not recorded on the legal definitive map in the next six years may be lost forever."

He shook his head sadly, and the rest of the table stopped their conversation to listen.

"We have a right to roam the land by law," the man continued, getting into his stride now while Marlene listened, nodding. "But greedy landowners are eager to make all parts of their land private. Our aim is to restore and register any historic public rights of way which are not yet shown on the definitive map. With Broomewode, the key is actually *using* the pathways, otherwise Lord Frome could apply for the pathway to close and we'd lose it forever. Plus, it would make it easier for him to shoot his way through the wild birdlife willy-nilly."

I'd had no idea that the pathway I'd taken so many times without thinking was such a hotbed of discussion. I was about to ask Marlene if her group had spotted the hawk when someone tapped me on the back.

It was Edward, the gardener. He was still wearing his work uniform and was holding a fizzing pint of cider. From the look on his face, he'd had a long day like me. He apologized for interrupting but said he couldn't help overhearing our conversation.

I looked behind where Edward was standing and saw that he'd been at a small table nearby alone. The other gardeners still hadn't welcomed him into the fold. I felt bad for him and told him to join us. Marlene gestured to a couple of spare stools, and we took a seat.

Edward took a sip of his cider and then introduced himself to Marlene and the others. "I get your point about rights of way," he said to the group. "But you also have to understand that we've been raising pheasant and grouse in these parts for centuries—with the sole aim of shooting them. It provides many people in rural areas with employment. Not to mention how it helps to control the natural order of wildlife."

Uh-oh. I could see Marlene turning pink and knew she was about to give him a mouthful. "Natural order of wildlife?" she sputtered.

"I hadn't thought about local jobs," I said quickly.

Edward sighed. "Working as a beater saved me from getting involved in any mischief as a young lad. I've been living in Devon since I was sixteen, but I grew up about an hour from Broomewode Village."

I coughed. How had I not known this? I'd thought Edward was a complete outsider, but he had early childhood ties here—just like me. Was his family still in Broomewode? I was burning with questions. Unfortunately for me, Edward seemed set on going down memory lane.

"When I was a young lad, one of my da's friends invited me along to a hunt as a beater to reload guns and help with the game. We'd be given a little money, a couple of grouse at the end of the day, and the earl would buy everyone a drink in the pub."

At this, Marlene snorted and I giggled. It was hard to imagine the earl being generous.

"That's only because Mitty was such a nice chap," Marlene said. "He would have put the earl up to that."

I asked who Mitty was, and Edward told me that he was the former gamekeeper.

"His family has lived in Broomewode for generations, and he was raised to respect the land," Marlene continued.

My heart began to race. Was this Mitty guy still in

Broomewode? If so, maybe I could talk to him about Valerie. Maybe he'd even known my dad?

"The gamekeeper position at Broomewode comes with a cottage tied to the job," Marlene continued. "Mitty's father did the job before him, and his father did it before him. They were good people."

"And the present earl treated him well," Edward added. "Mitty retired with a *very* generous pension after he had a stroke. He needs a lot of care, so now his lovely retirement home is all paid for by the earl."

I felt my face fall. Poor Mitty. Would his memories be hazy after the stroke? If so, he wouldn't be able to help me after all.

To my surprise, Marlene's eyes misted over. "I miss him," she said quietly. "He was a good friend. It's been far too long since I saw him. What home is he in? I'll visit next week. He may not remember me, but I know just how to get him talking about the old days and that will cheer him up." She stopped and took a sip of her tea. "Arthur isn't half the man his father was...and his own son is another terrible disappointment. Rumor is he's studying to be a dentist, so when Arthur moves on, the position will probably have to go to an outsider."

Edward chuckled. "A dentist? I bet that's wound up Arthur no end. It's the perfect comeuppance for that suck-up. Did you see how he dotes on the earl? All yes sir, no sir— doesn't question him for a second."

"So true!" I blurted out. Edward and Marlene looked at me in surprise. I paused for a moment, wondering how much I should say. But I could feel in my bones that these two ought to be allies. They'd have the same reaction as my coven sisters. "I saw the earl aim at a hawk yesterday."

"I told you he was a bad man," Marlene said, her eyes widening. "He has no right. Hawks are protected by the law. But I'm surprised you saw a hawk. We get a lot of white-tailed eagles around here, kestrels, and plenty of red kites. Are you sure it wasn't one of those?"

"I'm sure," I said. "It was a hawk, a big one. Very majestic. Is that unusual?"

Marlene nodded. I felt relieved. I'd definitely been seeing the same hawk then—and he *was* special.

Edward shook his head. "I wouldn't put it past the earl to shoot a hawk."

"Speak of the devil," Marlene said, pointing at the entrance to the pub. "There's his sidekick."

I turned and saw the earl's gamekeeper Arthur with a couple of young men who were obviously part of his hunting group. He was still wearing his hunting fatigues: wool cap, brown tweed jacket with matching vest, checked shirt, brown jodhpurs tucked into leather boots. He'd taken off his tie, and it was hanging from his jacket pocket. And, to my horror, his shotgun was tucked under his arm. He strode straight to the bar as if he owned the place.

Marlene's group sat up straight, outraged, and began whispering among themselves. To Edward and me, Marlene said, "He's not allowed in here with those weapons. The cheek of it."

"Like a fox storming the henhouse," Edward said.

"Well, I'm not going to sit here quietly. Today has been about making a point, and clearly we weren't loud enough."

Marlene stood, her chair scraping back loudly on the

stone floor. The rest of her group obediently followed, and Edward and me were left on our own.

Poor Edward. He was caught between a rock and a hard place. Clearly he thought Arthur was a buffoon, but he still had to work for the earl.

I laid a hand on his arm. "I think Marlene's got enough fight in her for all of us," I whispered.

Arthur and his men tried to order pints of ale from Eve, but she crossed her arms and shook her head. "You know full well you're not allowed in here with those wretched things." She pointed at Arthur's shotgun, which he'd leaned against the bar.

"I've no idea what you're talking about," he bellowed, laughing and looking to his friends with an exaggerated expression of confusion.

"What a child," I said to Edward. "Arthur has to be fifty at least. What's he playing the naughty schoolboy for?"

Edward rolled his eyes. "He's always like that. He's never gotten over his boarding-school antics."

I decided to show some solidarity to Eve and Marlene.

But it looked like I wasn't the only one determined to mess with Arthur and his crew.

Gerry had suddenly appeared by the bar, and I could see by his squashed-up concentrating face he was focused on trying to move the shotgun. I suppressed a giggle and went to stand by Marlene, who was in the middle of giving Arthur an earful.

"What on earth do you think you're doing, walking in here with a weapon?" she said. Even though Marlene was much shorter than Arthur and several decades older, she spoke as if she were looming over him, like he was a tiny spider she wanted to scare from the room.

Arthur laughed again, that awful facetious laugh of his. I could feel my blood boiling.

I looked out of the corner of my eye at Gerry. If his face could have turned red, it'd look like a British mailbox right now. He was making progress. The rifle began to lift ever so slightly from the floor. But Arthur was too focused on trying to make fun of Marlene to notice.

"It's not a weapon. It's a work tool," he said, emphasizing the syllables of "tool" as if Marlene might have trouble understanding him.

"I'm not hard of hearing," she snapped. "And all my wits are about me. Enough to know that bringing that thing in here is illegal. And wouldn't you know, I have a mobile phone in my back pocket. Present from the grandkids. Makes calling the police so easy, don't you think?" She slipped a brick of a phone from her pocket.

Again, Arthur laughed. "Honestly, after today's performance, I would have thought you'd be tired of embarrassing yourself." He made a show of checking his watch. I did the same. It was six p.m. Argh. Arthur was a meanie. I was about to step in, but one of Marlene's group got there before me. He was taller than Marlene and looked to be around the same age but with a full head of black hair.

"We might have ten or so years on you, Arthur, but we've got more common decency in our little fingers than you have in your whole body. Have you no shame? You know the earl stretches the limits of what he's legally allowed to hunt *and* tries to keep the public from their right to ramble, but you're too busy sucking up to his lordship to tell right from wrong."

At that, Arthur's phony smile dropped from his face. "Do you really have nothing better to do than go around slandering people you barely even know?"

"Oh, cut the crap, Arthur," Marlene retorted. "We've known you since you were in nappies."

Arthur was about to respond, but Gerry had been practicing his new talents.

"WHAT?" Arthur barked, looking frantically about the room. "Who's got my rifle?"

Gerry was grinning. He'd managed to lift the rifle and then laid it to rest on the other end of the bar. I was flabbergasted. How had I not noticed the thing moving? How had *no one* noticed? I had to hand it to Gerry—his skills were refined. Even if they were a bit risky.

"Where is it?" Arthur repeated.

Well, I certainly wasn't going to help him out.

Arthur and his friends began to hunt about until one of them noticed the rifle. He collected it from the other end of the bar and handed it back to Arthur.

He looked down at it in surprise. A vein was popping on his forehead, and beads of perspiration were stuck to the tufts of graying hair at his temples. "Cancel those pints, Eve," he said. "I've suddenly lost my thirst." He tucked his rifle underneath his arm again and turned to Marlene. "I don't know how you managed to do that, but you stay away from me. I've got my eye on you."

Marlene shook her head and poked her bony finger at his chest. "No, Arthur. I've got *my* eye on *you.*"

CHAPTER 11

"Ŵhat do you think, Poppy? Good idea?"

I came to and realized that Florence was waiting for an answer. To what? I'd been miles away, my thoughts caught up in Marlene's story about the old game-keeper. I couldn't stop myself from wondering if he'd recognize me like the old woman had in the pub the very first evening I came to Broomewode.

"You've no idea what I just asked, do you?" Florence laughed and shook out her curls. "Do you want to split the garlic baked camembert with me, or are you going to force me to be a greedy guts and gobble up the whole thing myself?"

The bird-watchers had left the pub shortly after Arthur and his crew, and Hamish had secured our usual table for dinner. Everyone was poring over the evening's menu, ravenous after a long day. Florence was the only one in good spirits, as well she might be after her double win. The rest of us were more subdued. We'd each faced our own difficulties during filming, and there was a palpable feeling of tension in the air, rather than the usual relief at the end of the first day.

I looked at each of the contestants' faces and wondered what it really meant to them deep down to win. Was it a matter of pride, or did they have their own set of personal reasons for being here like I did? It struck me that I knew very little about their motivations. A flash of shame came over me. I'd been so busy pursuing my own path. It was time to be more present. And then I realized Gaurav was missing. I was about to ask where he was when Florence waved her hand in front of my face.

"I'll split it, I'll split it," I said, laughing. "Sounds delicious."

"Honestly, Poppy, if only I had a pound for each time you got this dreamy look on your face and tuned out," Hamish said. "I could pay off my farm."

I laughed and promised to give my full attention to the cheese appetizer coming our way. I scanned the menu and decided to splurge on a steak. "Medium-rare, please," I said to Eve, who'd come over to take our order. She smiled at me and nodded.

"Where's Gaurav?" I asked.

Florence shook her head at me like I was being spectacularly dense. "Take a look over there." She swiveled in her seat and pointed to the pub's coziest corner, where Gaurav was sitting with Katie, the bridesmaid he'd met last weekend. They were sitting so close, their knees were touching, and Gaurav looked attentive as Katie talked. Watching them, I was filled with a warm feeling.

I turned back to Florence. "How lovely."

"I'm glad someone is finding romance," Florence said. "I shan't feel sorry for myself, dateless, on a Saturday night."

"You're not on a date; that's true," Hamish said, "but you did win today's competition hands down. So no complaining. Anyway, if you want a date, no doubt Darius is about. Or the new security man will be only too happy to show you a good time."

At that, Florence actually blushed. Hamish was right. She was never short of admirers. I accepted a glass of white wine and took a sip.

"Are you jealous, Pops?" It was Gerry, back again and floating now between Hamish and Florence, making a heart shape with his fingers and thumbs. Had he not exhausted himself with his little shotgun trick earlier? "I always thought you and Gaurav would make a cute couple."

I nearly choked on my wine. I liked Gaurav a lot but not in a romantic sense. And why was everyone so interested in my love life? After my experience with the cupid statue last week and bearing witness to a ruined wedding, a boyfriend was the last thing on my mind. I was determined to be a regular contestant on the show—no more going off on my own expeditions and certainly not chats with the dearly departed.

I cleared my throat and turned to Daniel, who seemed to be more quiet than usual. Daniel admitted that he was missing his kids, and he showed me some photographs on his phone, laughing at their array of silly poses.

As dinner arrived and we tucked into our meals, I thought how nice it was just having a normal Saturday night. No drama. Just interesting conversation, getting to know people better, and enjoying a delicious meal. I even felt like a dessert and joined Maggie in indulging in a sherry trifle.

By the time we'd finished stuffing ourselves, I was ready for an early night. I wondered where Gateau had got to—I wanted to snuggle up and read through my recipe for tomorrow one last time.

Eve brought us the bill, and as we settled up, I vowed to make sure I enjoyed more calm evenings like this in the future.

"I'm about ready to turn in," I said on a yawn.

But before anyone answered me, the strangest sound came from outside.

"What on earth was that?" I asked, feeling the hairs rise on the back of my neck. "It sounded like a woman's scream."

Hamish laughed. "It's just an owl. They make an awful racket."

Maggie shook her head. "That wasn't an owl. That was cats fighting."

But a sinking feeling spread through my belly. "That didn't sound like any animal I've heard."

Crack. Crack. Crack.

I jumped out of my seat. "That was a gunshot. I heard it yesterday when the earl was out shooting."

The color drained from Hamish's face. "Why would the earl be shooting now? It's getting dark. No point hunting in fading light."

What if he'd returned for the hawk? I couldn't let anything happen to that beautiful bird. I wished that I could explain why the bird meant so much to me, but for now, I'd have to appeal to Hamish's own interests. "Is it possible the earl and his gamekeepers are out shooting owls? Owls probably hunt small grouse too, right?"

But Hamish shook his head. "Not only is it getting dark, it's illegal to shoot an owl."

Florence stood and put an arm around my shoulders. "I know we've had some dramatics over the last few weeks, but not every bump in the night is something bad. What you think is gunshots is probably a car backfiring. And what you think is a scream is just an owl's hoot, like Hamish said. Trust him—he knows more about wildlife than any of us."

But I wasn't convinced. What if the earl had revenge in his heart and *was* taking another pop at the hawk? They hunted at night, didn't they?

"I'm just going to put my mind at ease," I said, "and make sure the earl isn't getting away with murdering more wildlife."

"Poppy, I say this as your friend. You should really stay out of things that don't concern you. You don't want the earl as an enemy. What if he finds out that you've been interfering and does something to get you voted off the show?" Florence's eyes were wide with concern, and I could see she had my best interests at heart. But what could I say? Sorry, but I'm worried the earl is shooting at a hawk that might be connected to my birth dad?

Gerry appeared behind her and said, "Or he might shoot you. Then where would you be?"

Thanks, Gerry.

I shrugged. "I'm going for a post-dinner walk. Not even the earl could object to that. Besides, I need to visit a local farm for some more eggs." I'd planned a visit before filming started tomorrow, but they didn't need to know that.

"I thought you wanted an early night," Hamish scolded. "I agree with Florence. You have to be careful with people like the earl."

I promised them I'd keep my wits about me and said my good nights—including to Gerry, whose mischievous streak hadn't been satisfied by his rifle trick and was now moving the salt shaker around on some poor couple's table.

OUTSIDE, the evening had turned cooler and I shivered in my shirtdress. The sky had a pink glow as the sun set. The air had a crisp quality to it, and I stood for a moment, inhaling deep.

I stepped onto the path that led to the manor house. It didn't seem like anyone was around. Was Florence right? Had a car just backfired in the parking lot and I was jumping to conclusions? Under my breath, I cursed the earl for distracting me from my good intentions of an early night. The minute I decided to focus on baking, the earl was distracting me. Again.

But was it really all the earl's fault? I knew I could be stubborn when I got a whiff of something strange, but there was also this feeling inside of me, like something was beckoning me, drawing me to investigate. I was following a sound, but it was more than that. Something intrinsic to my being. I was sure it was the hawk. Maybe it wasn't my business, but I had to investigate.

I headed towards the manor house, staying on full alert for any strange sounds, like shots. But there was a kind of gray silence to the evening, a flat line only broken by an occasional chirping bird I couldn't identify. I tried to empty my mind of its swirling thoughts, quiet it the same way the day had quieted. But I couldn't help returning to the image of my dad from the magic circle and his warning: *Listen to me carefully: You must leave this place. There are those who would do you harm.* Was the earl someone who was trying to do me harm? I shivered and then touched the amethyst necklace. I thought of all my sisters adding their power to help keep me safe. I was protected. I didn't need to be afraid.

I looked to the sky, hoping to see the hawk soaring high above me, graceful and free from the earl's bullets. I remembered what Susan had told me about hawks, how they're associated with good luck, clarity, and rising above bad situations so you can see the big picture. What did the hawk see from its vantage point up there? He had the best access to the big picture—if only I could see things through his eyes.

I turned the corner, and there was the manor house. All was still, but then I saw a shadowy figure emerging from behind a hill. Was it Arthur or one of his men? I sped up, heading straight for the figure to give them a piece of my mind. But then a happy bark broke my stride. I stopped and squinted into the distance. It was Sly, and Susan was a few yards behind him.

I called out a hello and jogged towards them.

Susan was dressed far more sensibly than I was, wearing a pair of brown jodhpurs and a cashmere sweater, her short hair brushed away from her face. She was smiling. "Poppy, how strange. I was just thinking about you. How did today go?"

I bent down to give Sly a few hearty strokes and explained that, in fact, I'd been on my way to see her for some more happy eggs after a mediocre day's baking. I'd need to pull out the stops tomorrow. Sly rubbed against me, his tongue hanging out. It was hard to feel gloomy when he was around.

"I heard some strange noises at dinner, and I thought maybe the earl or one of his gamekeepers were out hunting something they shouldn't be."

The smile on Susan's face dropped. "I do hope that's not the case. And if they tried, let's believe our protection spell spoiled their aim."

"I'm not sure it worked quite the way we were expecting it to," I said grimly. But before I could say anything more, another loud *craaaaaack crack crack* echoed through the air. Sly barked wildly, and Susan's brows shot up in alarm.

"Definitely gunshots, right?" I asked. I wasn't country-bred, but it sounded like gunfire to me.

She nodded and seemed to be listening to the air. "I've got a feeling that's coming from near the gamekeeper's cottage."

"We have to investigate," I said. "What if it's the earl and he's after the hawk again?" I cared about all the wild birds, but I really had a strong feeling about that hawk.

Susan nodded. "Come, I'll lead the way. I know a shortcut. But stay alert. We don't want to walk into the line of fire."

I gulped. No thanks. Eyes and ears would stay on high alert. And I was thankful to have Sly by my side. He'd helped keep me from danger in the past. Sure enough, he began acting like a herder, running just ahead of Susan and then behind me and back again, keeping his small flock safe.

Susan picked up the pace, a determined look on her face. "I swear, if Robert has harmed that hawk..."

"Robert?" I asked.

"Lord Frome."

"I forget he has a first name," I confessed, "and that you're on a first-name basis."

"Robert helped me and my late husband when we most needed help, and for that, I'll always be thankful. He's been good to me, too, since I've been widowed, but it doesn't mean I agree with everything he does. Not by a long shot." She mimicked cocking a rifle.

I matched her long gait, and Sly stayed close. Fury bubbled inside of me, and I was prepared to launch an angry tirade at whoever was out hunting and flagrantly flouting the rules. Susan made a sharp turn onto another footpath and led us away from the forest and towards the cottage I'd discovered by accident yesterday. We walked quickly and in silence. The light was going here amongst the trees so I was careful to stay close and try to make out the path ahead.

I heard rustling in the undergrowth and thought of all the life here on this property. It wasn't right that the earl and his sleazy sidekick should think they could kill anything they wanted to.

"We'll stop him," I blurted out.

She turned and flashed me a wary smile. "I just hope we're not too late."

Before long, the cottage came into view, its pale cream stone glowing in the fading light. There were the little windows framed in black with lead piping crisscrossing the glass. All the windows were shuttered. But whereas yesterday I'd coveted the cottage, admiring its original features and old-world charm, now there was something creepy about the place. I couldn't put my finger on what had changed, but I felt a weird charge of energy race through me as if it was trying to push me away from the scene.

I swallowed hard.

"What is it?" Susan asked softly as I put a warning hand on her arm.

"Something's not right. I can feel it."

At that, Sly began barking wildly. Susan bent to calm him. "What is it, boy, what is it?" she murmured. He panted for a moment as if gathering his breath and then raced towards the cottage.

Susan and I followed cautiously, conscious of walking straight into the path of danger.

But as we got closer, Sly suddenly stopped near the left side of the cottage and began barking loudly again.

Cold dread took over my body, and I began to sweat. Something was very wrong here. And then the air that had felt so fresh and cleansing earlier turned putrid. I wrinkled my nose. "Can you smell that?" I asked Susan.

"Smell what?"

"Something sour, something rotten."

She shook her head. "Come on," Susan said. "We'll look together."

We headed towards Sly, and I saw a shape. Something glinted on the ground. I went closer, dread filling my belly. "Oh, no," I cried when I made out that the shape was human, sprawled on the ground and not moving.

Susan gasped and clapped a hand to her mouth.

"Who...who is it?" she whispered.

Somehow, I found the strength to go closer. Sly hung back, looking as sorrowful as I'd ever seen. An object lay on the ground next to the body, and I shuddered when I realized it was a pair of binoculars. That's what I'd seen glinting, the uncovered lenses, as though the owner had been looking through them when disaster struck.

I went closer and recognized Marlene, her long body prostrate. The padded vest she'd been wearing earlier was zipped up to the neck, her bucket hat lay beside her. I rushed to her side.

Had she been so busy bird-watching she'd tripped on a root? Maybe she'd hit her head on a rock and knocked herself out. "Marlene," I called softly as I fell to my knees beside her. But even as I tried to believe she'd fallen and stunned herself, I knew on some level it wasn't true. I could feel that her spirit was already gone. And that's when I saw the wet darkness that had to be her life's blood.

Even though I knew it was hopeless, I bent to check Marlene's pulse. Her skin was still warm, her face slack. No pulse. No breath. She looked surprised, as though death had been a shock. Her fingers curled over the wound in her chest.

Susan raced over to my side. "Is she?"

I raised my head and realized that my eyes had filled with tears. "Yes. And by the looks of it, she's been shot. Shot dead."

CHAPTER 12

"Her name is Marlene," I said to Susan, who was on the phone to the police. "Marlene Applebaum," I added softly.

Susan repeated what I'd said into her mobile, trying to talk as calmly as she could. We were both spooked. Night had fallen. Twinkling stars appeared, but they made me feel like thousands of pairs of eyes were looking down on me, judging me. I tilted my face to look at the moon, a sliver smaller than it had been yesterday, and a cold feeling came over me. I'd asked the coven to help me protect the wildlife, and then Marlene and her wild bird society turned up the very next day, protesting. What if I'd dragged Marlene into my battle against the earl? Was it because of me she was dead?

"Poppy?" Susan said, her voice filled with urgency.

I realized she'd been asking me a question.

"The police are on their way, but are you sensing something? Earlier, when you said the air was putrid, I couldn't smell anything, and I have a keen sense of smell. I wonder if a new power is emerging—a way to warn you about danger? Can you smell anything now?"

I shook my head. A new power? I hadn't gotten to grips with the powers I had already. "No, there's nothing in the air now. But I am worried. Someone just shot a woman dead, and we're out here, alone."

Susan nodded grimly. "We can't leave her. Not until the police arrive."

She stroked Sly, who was glued to her side. He knew that something terrible had happened.

Softly, she chanted,

> *Goddess of the night,*
> *By the moon's light*
> *On this terrible night,*
> *I call to thee to give us your might*
> *To protect Poppy, Susan, and Sly*
> *From the ground to the sky.*
> *So I will, so mote it be.*
> *So I will, so mote it be.*

As she chanted the words, my heartbeat slowed and my breathing regulated. My mind began to clear. What had happened here was a tragedy. But I knew I had to stay calm if I was going to help get justice for Marlene.

Susan's eyes flickered open. "The police asked if one of us could lead them to the spot, but I don't want us to separate. Not even to walk down the hill. We're stronger together. Is there someone we can call to help?"

I instantly thought of Hamish. He was a professional, after all, and always knew the best thing to do. But I'd left my phone charging in my room at the inn. I told Susan as much. "Okay," she said, "I'll go down to the inn and get him. You stay here with Sly for protection."

I shook my head. "It's too dangerous, Susan. What if the murderer is roaming the fields right now? I don't want anything to happen to you."

"I've got my powers, and I'll use magic if I have to," she replied, setting her mouth in a firm line. "I'll send Hamish to you and wait for the police."

I took her hands in mine and felt that jolt of electricity again. "Please, please be careful. I couldn't bear to lose a sister so soon after finding her."

"You too, little sister. Blessed be."

"Blessed be."

I watched her take off with a heavy heart. Sly stood and looked torn when he realized we were separating. Susan gave him a final pat and told him to stay. He barked once as if reporting for duty. "You're a good boy," I said softly.

As Susan's silhouette disappeared into the dark, I fought the urge to run after her. I couldn't let another woman come to harm. It hadn't been that long ago I'd heard the shots that presumably killed Marlene. Whoever had fired them must be close by. I turned and looked again at Marlene's still body. *Please, please don't let this be my fault.* It was then, alone by that cottage—the moon shining overhead, casting the hills in a shadowy shimmer—that the full force of my responsibilities really hit me.

I was a witch. A water witch. I had powers. And sisters. Women who needed me to be strong and in control. It wasn't just about me and my search for my birth family anymore; I was part of a community now. I had to be more in control of my powers.

"Poppy? You up there?"

Hamish ran down the path towards me, panting. I'd been so lost in my thoughts that I hadn't even heard him coming.

Zero out of ten for keeping your wits about you, Pops.

"Thank heavens you're okay," Hamish said. "Susan burst into the pub with an expression on her face that nearly made my heart stop. I thought something had happened to you."

Hamish put his arms around me in a bear hug. He smelled of warmth, fires and good food, like the pub. I inhaled and let myself be comforted—it was creepy as all hell out here, after all.

Sly seemed happy to see Hamish too, and he nuzzled against his foot.

But another voice broke us apart. "You're alive!"

It was Gaurav. Carrying a flashlight.

"I am, I am. Thank you both for rushing over here."

"Thought you might need a torch."

"Thanks, mate," Hamish said.

"She's over there," I said quietly.

Hamish followed my gaze. "Susan is waiting for the police. She said Marlene was shot."

"Yes. I had to check to see if she was alive, but I tried not to touch anything in case it's needed for evidence."

"Good thinking, Poppy," Hamish said. He took the flashlight and went closer to Marlene's body and squatted down. I averted my gaze, as I didn't want to see poor Marlene lit up.

"It was a shotgun," he said quietly.

Hamish turned back to the body. "She was shot with what you'd call buckshot."

I had so many questions, but I heard Susan's voice. She was with DI Hembly and Sgt. Lane. And, to my surprise, Benedict was with them, also carrying a flashlight.

DI Hembly greeted me with his brusque manner, all business. He was dressed for work. Sgt. Lane, on the other hand, looked like he'd been off-duty when the call came in. He was wearing jeans and a casual shirt, as was Benedict.

"She's over there," Susan said, pointing, and Hamish once more focused the beam of light on the dead woman.

Benedict took a step closer. "She looks familiar."

"Her name was Marlene Applebaum," I said.

"She was killed by a shotgun," Hamish added.

Benedict looked right at me. "Wasn't she one of the Somerset wild bird people? She's still got her binoculars. But what on earth was she doing out here at this time of night? And all alone?"

"I don't know. But she and her group had an argument with your father. They were trying to save their ancient rights of way."

Benedict's eyes opened so wide, I could see the whites gleam in the moonlight.

While Benedict took a moment to process that information, DI Hembly gave instructions to Sgt. Lane.

Hamish waited until he'd finished, then said, "There's something you should see, Detective Inspector." He pointed his flashlight beam to a spot on the ground behind us. Sgt. Lane went over, then got a plastic bag out of his pocket. He retrieved something, then came forward and showed us a shotgun cartridge he'd retrieved from the grass.

"That's from shooting magpies and crows," Benedict said. "It's perfectly legal."

Hamish said, "Birds would be shot with a light load. One ounce of shot. This cartridge is a heavy load. Almost two ounces."

"That's the size for a fox," Benedict said.

Hamish replied, "It's enough to take down a man." He glanced down at Marlene. "Or a woman."

I gulped. Having my suspicions confirmed wasn't always rewarding. There was foul play here, and now no one could deny it.

Sgt. Lane turned to me. "Susan told us you were out walking when you bumped into each other. But did you see anyone?"

"No," I said. I paused for a moment. "Wait. Yes. I saw a man, shadowy because it was getting dark. Near the manor house." What I was about to say could have some serious connotations. I didn't want to take them lightly. "But Marlene and her bird society were here earlier today. They were protesting. They believe the earl is trying to take back their ancient rights of way."

"This was today, you say?"

It seemed about a year ago, but it had only been a few hours. "Yes. They made so much noise, we had to stop filming the baking contest. Marlene was the ringleader. She and the new security guard clashed heads."

"And she had words with our director, Fiona," Gaurav added.

"But that was nothing compared to the argument she had with the earl yesterday," I told them.

Benedict said, "My father was only defending his rights as a landowner."

"And then I saw Marlene in the pub after we'd finished

filming for the day," I continued. "She was drinking tea with the other society members. That was only a couple of hours ago. It seems impossible she's dead."

Sgt. Lane scribbled away in his notebook, taking it all down.

"What were you doing here, Poppy?" DI Hembly asked.

"I was coming to see Susan to get some eggs for tomorrow. We heard someone shooting and came to see what was going on." I sounded as nosy and interfering as the earl no doubt considered the birders.

Susan said, "Seemed an odd time for someone to be shooting." I appreciated her support.

I said quietly, gesturing at Marlene, "Her skin was still warm when I checked for a pulse."

"Forensics will be able to tell us the exact time when death occurred. They're on their way," DI Hembly said. "But I agree. You may have heard the shots that killed her."

"If only we'd gotten here sooner," I said, almost to myself.

Sgt. Lane turned to Benedict, who looked like he'd seen a ghost.

"Where might we find the earl now, sir?" he asked.

"Don't be absurd," Benedict replied, pulling himself together. "I don't like what you're insinuating here. My father would never kill a woman on his land. Besides, he only uses Purdey shotguns and shot."

Hamish pointed to the bag still in the sergeant's hand. "That is Purdey shot."

CHAPTER 13

"*W*hat's going on here?"

By now I would recognize that pompous tone anywhere. It belonged to Arthur, the gamekeeper, who was returning home to a murder scene.

DI Hembly stepped forward and explained what had happened to Marlene, and I took the opportunity to give Arthur the once-over. He was in the same hunting tweeds I'd seen him in earlier, but he'd ditched the shotgun. He looked genuinely surprised at finding a group of police officers (and baking contestants) gathered near his property, and I watched as that surprise turned to disbelief and then horror. His features seamlessly arranged themselves into the right configuration. He was clearly someone who knew how to respond to bad news. Was that good schooling, or had he faced a lot of adversity in his time? Now that I knew he was the son of someone Marlene had liked and respected, I tried to soften my earlier judgment of him.

"That's terrible," Arthur said when DI Hembly finished. "I

was just out checking on the grouse chicks for the night. I didn't hear anything. You said she's been shot to death?"

"That's right," DI Hembly said. "I don't suppose you know where we could find the earl?"

"Now?" Arthur asked.

DI Hembly nodded.

"Whatever for?"

"We have some questions we'd like to ask him."

Was it my imagination, or did Arthur look genuinely worried about his boss?

"I have no idea where the earl might be. Try the big house."

"He means Broomewode Hall," Benedict chimed in. "But like I said earlier, my father would never do such a thing."

You would say that, Benedict.

Susan came closer to me. While the others talked, she said softly, "I can believe Robert would shoot birds of prey but not that he'd gun down a human being."

My mind traversed all its memories of the earl, flicking through each of our encounters like an old film reel: the first time we met, when I bluffed my way into the manor house, to the moment I caught him out hunting yesterday with that horrible smirk on his face as he raised his shotgun to the hawk. Could this reserved, uptight member of the aristocracy, so concerned with airs and graces and traditions, really have a much darker side?

It wasn't like murderers walked around wearing T-shirts with *Killer* in bold type across their chests. One thing I'd learned over the last month was that the most surprising people were capable of murder, given the right triggers.

The crime scene investigation team began to arrive, bringing lights and equipment.

DI Hembly asked if Benedict would accompany him and Sgt. Lane to Broomewode Hall to speak with the earl. Benedict obviously didn't want to but, with a shrug, led the way.

The detective inspector told me and Susan to return to the inn, where he'd come to take our statements later. We agreed, of course—as if I wanted to spend a moment longer at a murder scene in the middle of the dark countryside. Susan and Sly led the way, with Hamish and Gaurav following. I took one last look at the scene, now busy with experts who would try to find out what had happened to Marlene. I didn't see or feel her nearby so I imagined she'd passed on smoothly, at least.

I was sad to think of that determined woman having her life force snuffed out like that. There was some consolation knowing she'd moved on. I wondered if poor Gerry would ever find his way to the other side.

As I was about to turn, I saw a moving shadow above the gamekeeper's cottage. The hawk, I was sure of it. Probably I was in shock, but it seemed perfectly normal for me to raise my hand as though I were waving to an old friend.

When I joined the group, I didn't feel quite so terrible.

We were a silent group. Gone was the easy chatter between us. It wasn't like we could compare the best techniques for making puff pastry or poaching pears after an innocent old lady had been gunned down. Even Sly walked at a melancholy pace.

But our silence was broken by the sound of someone whistling tunelessly. As we grew closer to the inn, a shadowy figure came into view.

"Who's there?" Susan asked, her voice steady but with a tinge of trepidation creeping in.

"And why are they whistling 'Eye of The Tiger'?" Hamish added.

"Who are you? And what's your business here?" was the curt reply.

I let out a breath in relief. It was Martin, the overzealous security guard. He nearly blinded me when he directed a powerful flashlight beam on us all. His head of dark hair was styled in his usual severe parting, and he was wearing the gray security guard's uniform of smart trousers with a crease down the middle, walkie-talkie at the hip, and a short-sleeved shirt with the Broomewode crest. But for the second time this weekend, he was nowhere near the baking tent. Wasn't his job to guard the filming area, not ramble through the fields? Was Martin a renegade or just bad at his job?

Or could there be a more sinister explanation?

"Isn't that the security guard Florence was flirting with?" Hamish asked softly.

I told Hamish that it was the second time I'd seen him wandering around at night with no clear reason.

"Martin, it's Poppy. You know me. And Hamish and Gaurav from the baking show."

"Turn off the light, mate," Hamish said, putting a hand in front of his eyes.

"Can't be too careful," Martin said. "Thought I heard shots." He lowered the light but didn't turn it off. "And you spend an awful lot of time wandering around at night, Poppy."

"It helps me relax," I said. Not that it was any of Martin's business what I did. "Anyway, we're headed back to the inn now. Night." He watched us all the way.

When we arrived back at the pub, it was even busier than when I'd left. Though only an hour or so had passed, I had gone from determined to do well in my baking tomorrow to being determined to find out what had happened to Marlene.

Edward was still there, sitting at a table with some of the crew from the show, including Robbie, the sound guy. I caught snippets of their conversation, mostly grumbles about scenes that were going to have be reshot after the bird-watchers' antics earlier. Hearing that made me even sadder. They spoke of Marlene as if she'd been nothing but trouble, but all she'd wanted was to protect the countryside and the wild birds who called it home.

Hamish asked if I wanted a drink, but I needed my wits about me for my upcoming police interview. Besides, I was chilled to the bone, so I asked for a pot of tea.

I inched closer to the crew's table to hear more.

"So many shots were messed up," one of the cameramen was saying. "It's played havoc with the schedule. And that costs some serious money. I wouldn't want to be in Donald Friesen's shoes right now. That all comes down to him."

"That man is *always* stressed," Robbie said.

"If you want to get paid the big bucks, you have to be able to handle the big stakes," the cameraman said. "Him and Fiona should have got those pesky old age pensioners under control yesterday."

"Or hire better security guards," Robbie added. "That new one's hopeless."

Florence beckoned me over, and I abandoned eavesdropping and joined the group who were still there after all.

Florence, Daniel, Maggie and Amara were waiting at our usual table and gestured for us to sit down.

"What's going on? We've been so worried," Florence said in her usual dramatic fashion. "Susan came rushing in demanding Hamish, then Gaurav went running after him. Now you all look like you've seen ghosts."

"Ghosts?" Gerry suddenly appeared at my side. "Do I have company? Is it someone interesting?" He looked so pleased, I didn't have the heart to tell him that yet another spirit had passed on while he was still stuck here. Besides, I couldn't tell him anything without the others thinking I'd gone mad.

In truth, I didn't want to tell anyone that another innocent person had been murdered in Broomewode. Everyone was already on edge—especially Daniel, who'd had a difficult day baking. I didn't want to be the bearer of bad news.

Luckily, Hamish stepped up and explained what had happened. The bakers listened, wide-eyed and aghast.

"So you were right," Maggie said quietly. "You *did* hear gunshots earlier."

"I'm so sorry I thought you were overreacting." Florence smiled sadly. "Normally that's my job."

I assured her it was okay. I wished that I *had* been overreacting. But after seeing the earl and Arthur hunting yesterday, the noise of their shots had stayed with me. I'd recognize the sound anywhere.

Edward must have sensed the drama at our table because he excused himself from the crew's table and joined us, another half-pint of fizzing cider in his hand.

I took a deep breath and explained what had happened to Marlene.

Edward shook his head, and his blond hair fell over his eyes. "I don't understand. We were talking to her just a couple of hours ago. I thought she was going home."

What could I say? Edward was right. It was surreal. Too bizarre to really get my head around. Until yesterday, Marlene was a stranger to me. But this weekend, we'd crossed paths many times. Could that really have been a coincidence? Or were we supposed to have met? Could she have led me to more discoveries about my birth parents? I couldn't shake the feeling that her ties to Broomewode Village and the game-keeper position were a clue in the mystery of my search. I studied Edward's contemplative face—now that I knew that he'd been born in Broomewode, maybe he could tell me more about Marlene and the old gamekeeper.

And he was right. Why hadn't Marlene gone home?

"Before our chat today, had you met Marlene before?" I asked him.

He shook his head. "I'd seen her around. Remember talking to her at a fete once and my dad talking about her, but we'd never actually met. Dad was very sociable when we lived here. He knew a lot of local gossip."

At this I had to control my excitement. How could I orchestrate a meeting with Edward's dad? Yet another person who could perhaps shed light on my past.

"Back then, Marlene had been causing trouble with the local council about a new motorway they wanted to approve. But he said she wasn't a bad sort. Just a bit determined. Clearly nothing had changed over the years. She was a fire-cracker."

"Can you remember anything else?" I urged. "Any clue about Marlene's past could help the investigation."

Edward took a sip of his half-pint and then closed his eyes in concentration. "I don't know how helpful it is, but Marlene was a country-bred woman through and through. She always had it in for the current earl. She thought he ran the estate purely for profit. He wasn't country-bred, you see? Didn't respect the traditions. She couldn't forgive him that."

Before I could press him for any more information, two of the bird-watchers from Marlene's group walked into the pub, holding hands. They'd changed out of their daywear, and the woman was wearing a knitted dress with ballet pumps and the man a smart shirt and trousers. It was obviously date night, and by the look on their faces, one they'd been looking forward to. Had love bloomed over binoculars and wild birds?

They obviously didn't know about Marlene, and I didn't want to be the one who told them—I didn't have it in me to break their hearts. "They don't know," I said, feeling horrible.

But as they waved hello and looked around for a table, Edward put his hand on my arm and said softly, "Don't worry. I'll let them know."

I smiled gratefully. "Thank you," I whispered.

Edward spoke to the two bird-watchers in a soft, thoughtful tone. He handled the situation with such compassion and care that my heart almost melted on the spot. But as he spoke, the bird-watching couple looked sick to their stomachs.

"Poor Marlene," the woman said, coming up to me. "And you found her?"

"Yeah." Not something I'd ever forget.

"What an awful way to go."

Yes again.

"But when she left, I thought she was going home."

Seemed we all had. Why had Marlene changed her mind?

"Can you think of a reason why she'd go to Broomewode Hall? Or the gamekeeper's cottage?" I asked.

They looked at each other, and both shook their heads. "She must have heard or seen something. Marlene wasn't one to hold back if something was bothering her," the woman said. "Perhaps she went to have another go at the earl. She was that cross with him."

I nodded. "The police were asking if she had any enemies. Can you think of anyone that might have it in for Marlene?" Okay, the police hadn't asked that, but I knew they would soon enough.

The couple looked embarrassed.

"The thing is," the man began, clearing his throat before continuing, "Marlene had a good heart, but she rubbed people up the wrong way. And I mean a lot of people. Every hunting landowner in Somerset and anyone who had ever tried to take back public rights of way was her enemy."

"There are even a few in our society who think that she went too far," the woman added, glancing around to make sure no one could overhear. "Not us, though," she said quickly.

I wanted to ask more questions, but Gaurav gestured towards the entrance, where Sgt. Lane was standing, scribbling something in his notebook.

Edward asked if he could buy the couple a drink and toast to Marlene, and the three of them went to the bar, where Darius was frantically trying to serve the Saturday night crowd and flirt with Florence at the same time.

"Let's give our statements and then get ourselves to bed," Hamish said to me and Susan. "Tomorrow's going to be a long day."

I sighed. He wasn't wrong. And not just because we had to bake a showstopper.

CHAPTER 14

From my bedroom window, the moon was a gorgeous silver orb, casting the fields of Broomewode in a shimmering glow. A light breeze ruffled the red curtain, but otherwise all was still and quiet. No birds, no chatter from people idling outside, no traffic. No crack of a shotgun. It was as if the normal hustle and bustle of life had been suspended and in its place was a silent reverence for Marlene's passing. The scene was so beautiful, it seemed cruel.

I was fairly certain her spirit had made it over to the other side, though I wasn't always right. Sometimes it took a while for spirits to appear to me. Marlene was a prime case for some worldly lingering—she'd spent her life fighting for causes she believed in, and she'd been robbed of the opportunity to see them through. Would unfinished business keep her on this plane? She'd been a woman on a mission, that was for sure, determined and single-minded, and from what her fellow bird-watchers had said, she'd made quite a few enemies along the way. But all she wanted was to save wild birds and their habitat. She had respect for nature, and in turn, I respected Marlene.

As I stared out of the window, sleepless, I couldn't bear the idea that her murderer was out there somewhere, walking free on the land she fought so hard to protect.

I knew I had a big day tomorrow, but I couldn't settle. Sleep seemed like a distant idea—my thoughts were too entangled with the dead. They turned from Marlene to my birth dad, who I was pretty certain had been appearing to me as a ghost. I hadn't really had time to process that realization. I'd been too caught up in deciphering his warning and trying to save the hawk that I felt was somehow linked to him to really wrap my head around his passing. Now I was filled with a gloomy, empty feeling. I'd never known my birth dad, had no clue as to his identity or whereabouts, no idea what he might look or sound like in real life. But now that he had appeared to me, it was like he was suddenly in reach for the first time. Except I'd seen enough ghosts to know that he was among them. It didn't seem fair.

Gateau sensed my despair and raised her head. She'd been napping on her favorite chair, curled into a croissant-shaped ball on the soft red cushions, but now she leapt onto the windowsill and nuzzled against me. I scratched behind her ears and felt soothed by her gentle purrs of appreciation.

But questions still filled my head. What had happened to my dad? He must have been pretty young when he died. Katie Donegal had told me that my mom went to London on weekends, and for a while I'd considered that my dad might have lived there, that perhaps they'd been having a long-distance romance. But since seeing his ghost here in Broomewode, I'd rejected this idea. I could feel in my gut that my dad was a local.

"How will I find my dad if he's dead?" I asked aloud.

"There'd be a record somewhere," a voice said behind me. Gateau arched her back and promptly stopped purring.

Gerry!

I turned to find my ghostly sidekick sitting cross-legged in the middle of my bed.

"But I don't know his name or anything about him."

Gerry looked at me like I was a couple of eggs short of a meringue. "How many young blokes die here in any year? That is, when you're not around."

So far, getting any information out of the Broomewode locals had been nearly impossible. When it came to the subject of the past, they either clammed up or had a selective memory. Katie Donegal, the cook at Broomewode Hall, had helped me, but she was definitely holding back. She obviously knew more than she was telling me about my birth mom. I was certain there were other older people in the area who might know my father, but I kept coming up empty-handed. Maybe Gerry was right. If I was ever going to get answers about my dad, I was going to have to conduct my own research into locals who'd died in the last twenty-five or so years.

Since most people who died tended to be older, there couldn't be too many, could there?

The silence of the night was broken as Marlene's bird-watching friends made their way out of the inn and around the side path. I watched as their silhouettes were swallowed up by the dark, two loving bodies walking slowly, arm in arm. Once upon a time, that exact image would have belonged to my parents, walking around Broomewode Village, bound by that inexplicable feeling that brings two strangers together, compels them to discover all they can about each other, to trust each other, to fall in love. Or had it not worked that way for them? Had their relationship been a secret, conducted behind closed doors? Were they always afraid of being caught? And if that was the case, then why?

Even now, there was so much distance between the watery visions my mom used to communicate with me and the appearances of my dad in the magic circle. Why did they never appear to me together? Had something, or someone, created a gulf between them? And if my mom was alive, then why all the cloak and daggers? She knew where I was—why not visit me in person? Surely it would be less distracting than using water as her conduit?

"Gerry, I think you might be right. I've been waiting for other people to give me information, and all I get is half-truths and cryptic warnings. Yes. It's time I did some digging. Good work."

"Thanks." He flipped a few times, then settled himself again. "Not to mention that I saved your cake today."

"You did. And I'm sorry I couldn't thank you properly. There've always been people around."

"And what's this about a new ghost in town?" he asked, looking eager. "Is she young and hot?"

I was going to call him on wanting anyone young and hot to die just so he could have the company but stopped myself in time. The last thing I needed was a reminder that Gerry had also been young and hot (at least in his own mind). I said, "Of course you want company. But I don't think you'd like Marlene. Anyway, I haven't seen her since..."

"Since she died." He put his chin in his hand. "Why haven't I gone anywhere?"

"I don't know." I felt bad for him, stuck between worlds, and tried to cheer him up. "Maybe it's because I need you." Really, I was only being nice, but it was true that Gerry had his uses. He could drift through walls and doors, eavesdrop without being detected, and even his new talent of moving objects might come in handy.

He didn't look as gratified as I'd hoped. "Can't keep me here for your own selfish ends, Pops."

"I know. I'm sorry. While I'm researching my dad, I'll see if I can figure out how to help you on your way."

"Appreciate it."

"In the meantime, spend as much time as you can in the pub. Everyone will be gossiping about Marlene's murder by tomorrow. What are they saying? Everyone has secrets. What were Marlene's?"

"When I was on the listen before, when she was talking about the gamekeeper's old dad, I thought she sounded like she was fond of the old boy. Is there a secret there?"

"You're right. Maybe she had a crush on him. And I'd be killing two birds with one stone—which Marlene definitely wouldn't approve of! I wonder if Mitty remembers anything about Valerie and my father? He's in a care home after having a stroke." I knew that people who'd had a stroke often struggled with their memory recall. But perhaps he'd remember more about the past than the recent present, the same way it worked with dementia. With a little sleuthing, I could find out where he was—and ask him about Marlene, the many enemies she gathered over the years, and also about any local young men who'd died in the last twenty-five years. Surely there couldn't be that many? If my mom *was* alive, he might also know of her whereabouts. I didn't even notice Gerry float toward the window until Gateau screeched.

"Can you please stop that thing from hissing at me," Gerry muttered, settling himself in Gateau's favorite chair.

"If you stop tormenting her," I retorted, trying to calm my wriggling familiar. But she leapt from my arms and out through the window. Her little tail was the last thing to disappear as she hopped along the drain gutter and down to the ground floor.

I turned back to Gerry, who was back relaxing on my bed, now stretched out, legs crossed at the ankle. "Just because you're a spirit doesn't mean you can put your shoes on my bed," I chastised.

Gerry laughed and floated over to the window. We stood like that for a moment, both looking into the distance. For once, Gerry seemed to be lost in thought rather than interested in goofing around. I took in his red spiky hair, the shirt pattered with cars and trucks. No doubt he'd have made some different choices if he'd known he'd be wearing that shirt in the afterlife. "I promise that as soon as this competition is over, I'm going to help you find a way to the other side," I said quietly.

Gerry stayed silent but nodded. "It's not like I don't have my fun here—the trick with that twerp's shotgun earlier was a blast, ha ha, but that can't be all there is, can it?"

I shook my head. "I don't know what the other side holds, but I'm hopeful that it's peaceful." The image of my dad came back to me. For his sake, I hoped it was more than peaceful—I hoped it was blissful. I turned to Gerry and told him about my dad's appearance. "Have you seen him around?"

"No. As far as I can tell, I'm the only ghost between here and the tent." He sighed. "And once that tent comes down, I'll have even less fun than I do now."

"We'll figure this out. I'm sure we will."

Gerry smiled. "You should get some rest. Big day tomorrow. I need you to make it back here next week, remember?"

He wished me good night and floated through the door. Gerry was right. I needed a good sleep if I was going to bake a showstopper worthy of the name tomorrow. But I was also going to get up early. Before filming started, I had a call to make. Katie Donegal was going to receive a visitor in the Broomewode Hall kitchen. This time I'd find a way to make her talk.

CHAPTER 15

I hugged my cardigan to my ribs as I climbed the
path to Broomewode Hall. I'd left Gateau sleeping
at the foot of my bed (she'd obviously had a big night doing
cat things) and had only crawled back through the window as
I was leaving. It was like sharing a room with a teenager.

I'd delayed breakfast, too, afraid of catching any early
risers who might question (rightly) where I was off to so
early on a Sunday morning before filming. My stomach
growled angrily, but as soon as I'd spoken with Katie Donegal, then I'd fill it with some scrambled eggs and bacon.
This is what it'd come to—I was bartering with my own
appetite.

By now, my feet found their own way to Broomewode
Hall, and I walked on autopilot, my mind focused on the best
way to get Katie Donegal to open up to me. There was something she was afraid of, but I couldn't put my finger on what.
Had something tragic happened in her past? Was she afraid
of the earl? I shivered as I pictured Lord Frome aiming his
shotgun at the hawk—the look of intense concentration, his

144

focus on killing. Had DI Hembly and Sgt. Lane gotten anywhere with their inquiries last night?

I was itching to know if the earl had been involved in Marlene's death—after all, I was about to knock on his back door. But even if there was personal drama at the manor house, I was determined to get some answers in my personal drama. In her honor, I was taking a leaf out of Marlene's book and would stand my ground stubbornly until I got what I wanted.

But as the old manor house came into view, some of my resolve weakened. Even after all these weeks, the big stone hall still managed to impress and intimidate me, especially in the morning when it glowed gold. The flowerbeds were spilling over, abundant with blooms, and the lawns had that military precision I'd come to expect from Edward and the other gardeners.

Keep focused, Pops, I commanded myself. *You've got a job to do here.*

I headed towards the northwest side of the house and the staff entrance by the kitchen. For a split second I hesitated, unsure if I was about to encounter the wrath of the whole household for telling the police Marlene and the earl had argued yesterday, but I calmed myself down.

Everyone on the set had seen Marlene and her cronies breaking the quiet and interrupting filming. And I suspected half the village knew about Marlene and the earl's mutual dislike. Besides, the Champneys wouldn't be caught dead in the kitchen with the staff. They'd never know I'd even been there.

I swallowed, took a deep breath and then rang the bell and waited for someone to let me in.

"One moment, please," a voice called from the hallway. I didn't recognize who it belonged to, and my heart began to thump.

But when the door swung open, it was the cook I'd seen at the magic circles. She had shiny black hair tied in a bun at the nape of her neck, dark, lively eyes, and a broad smile. She was probably not that much older than me, twenty-eight or twenty-nine, and her olive skin looked soft to the touch, like velvet, with a smattering of freckles across her nose.

"Oh, it's you," she said, slipping an arm around my shoulders and ushering me inside. I felt that familiar zing of connection, but the current wasn't as strong as with Susan, Eve or Elspeth. I wondered if age or experience affected the current in your body. "I've been waiting for a chance to talk to you," she continued. "Somehow you've managed to capture the attention of the great Elspeth Peach. You are a lucky thing," she said good-naturedly.

I didn't know how to respond, so I mumbled something about how much I admired Elspeth.

"I haven't even introduced myself yet, and here I am blabbing on. I'm Belinda."

"Poppy," I replied.

We entered the kitchen. There was no one else there. It was strange to see the room devoid of hustle and bustle, nothing bubbling away on the stove. Belinda noticed me looking and said, "There's only two of us on this morning. There are no events or company this weekend, only the three of them to cook for, so she gave most of the kitchen staff the day off. Sit, sit." She pointed at a stool by the table. "Have a cup of tea."

Belinda had one of those voices that was as welcoming and warm as it was commanding. I sat down and wondered how quickly I could ask about Katie Donegal without seeming rude. Had she gone off again right when I wanted to talk to her? As nice as this was, I hadn't dragged myself out of bed to have a cozy chat. I was here for the facts.

A kettle whistled, and Belinda poured boiling water into a pretty teapot patterned with red poppies. She brought the pot and three matching teacups over to the table. "Katie will be down in a minute, so we don't have much time to talk." She leaned forward, her dark eyes warm and smiling, and lowered her voice. "I've so many questions for you, Poppy." She clasped her hands in her lap, her pristine white apron rippling. "Like, have you just found out that you're a witch? Have you discovered your powers yet? Which element are you? I'm earth."

I laughed, my mood lifted now that I knew Katie Donegal was on her way. And there was something about Belinda I instantly warmed to.

"I'll answer in order," I said, still laughing. "I found out I was a witch about a month ago. I'm water. And I'm just starting to discover my powers."

"Oooh, that's the best bit," she whispered excitedly. "You're at the beginning of an amazing journey."

She took my hands, and I felt the charge course through my fingertips. I was about to ask about Belinda about her own journey when the sound of singing sent shivers down my spine. The voice was lilting and gentle, the melody so familiar, it was as if I'd written it myself.

I know where I'm going,
And I know who's going with me.
I know who I love,
And the dear knows who I'll marry.

"That's Katie. She's always singing or humming," Belinda said. "Makes the work easier, she says. We'll have to talk later."

I could only nod in response. My whole body went cold. This was the song Valerie was singing in my second vision by the lake last week. I knew the words. Every line. For so long, the lyrics had been buried inside me somewhere, long forgotten. But I'd found that I knew every word.

The singing was getting louder.

I have stockings of silk
And shoes of bright green leather,
Combs to buckle my hair
And a ring for every finger.

"More later," Belinda whispered and got up from the table. But I couldn't move. I was shaken to the core. Why was Katie singing the same song as my mom? Had she taught my mom the words? If they'd been close enough to sing with each other, why had Katie pretended she barely knew her? Surely it couldn't be a coincidence that they knew the same song, that *I* knew the song...that it had been sung to me when I was a baby.

Katie walked into the kitchen, humming now rather than singing. She looked lost in her own world. Each time I saw her, I was taken aback by how small she was, only around five feet, with alert green eyes. She was still in her cast but was obviously on the mend. When she saw me, Katie immediately stopped singing, and a flash of surprise shot across her face.

"Poppy," she said. "Hello, dearie. Nice to see you." She smiled broadly, but her forehead twitched, and she began stroking the nail of her little finger. Why did I make her so nervous?

"Good morning, Katie. What a pretty song."

"Shouldn't you be in the tent this morning, dearie, baking something wonderful?"

"Not for a couple of hours," I said. "I was hoping to have a quick chat."

"With me?"

I nodded. "I'm afraid something terrible happened yesterday, but I think you might be able to help."

She nodded solemnly. "I think I know what you're talking about."

Belinda looked at me quizzically but excused herself. "I have to start setting the dining table for breakfast," she said. I inwardly thanked her for her discretion.

When Katie entered, I'd stood to greet her, but now she gestured back at the stool. I poured a cup of tea into the cup Belinda had left out, added a splash of milk, then passed it to her. She thanked me.

"This is just the ticket," she said, taking a sip. "I didn't get much sleep last night."

"Me either." I was dying to ask Katie more about the song she'd been singing, but I feared that would only scare her off.

Instead, I kept things light and asked how she was managing with her arm, if it kept her up at night. She shook her head no, that she was on the mend. "The lack of sleep isn't down to me poor arm. It's just that the police were here last night. Caused a dreadful commotion, though His Lordship and Her Ladyship acted as if it were nothing at the time. They interviewed the earl about poor Marlene."

"You knew her?"

"Oh yes, Marlene was the kind to make herself known round here."

At that I smiled. It certainly matched the image of the woman I'd briefly met.

"I didn't know her well," Katie continued, "but she was a thorn in the earl's side. They didn't see eye to eye, not to speak ill of the dead. But she did get on with the former gamekeeper, Mitty, which was strange considering how he earned his living."

"Do you know where the old gamekeeper's living? Marlene said something about a posh care home."

"Yes, that's right. The poor thing had a stroke. I don't recall the name of the home, but it's in a town not far away. In Chippenham, I think." She leaned closer. "She might not think much of the new earl, but it's him who pays the hefty fee to keep Mitty in his comfortable home."

"That's nice," I said, thinking it was the least the earl could do after the man had given a lifetime's service. I wondered if Marlene had managed to visit the old gamekeeper yesterday before she was murdered. It was about a half-hour drive from the inn, so the timing was possible. If she had, maybe he might remember something about his old friend that could help the case. If he'd had a stroke, might he still be able to communicate?

"Poor Marlene," Katie repeated, shaking her head. "Shot to death. What a way to go. Though what that had to do with the earl, I don't know. After the police left, there was a great row of which I've never heard the likes of before. The earl and Benny were shouting at each other. I couldn't make out the words exactly, but it was the tone which stuck with me. Pure fury. It was chilling. Then Lady Frome stepped in, tried to cool things down—no doubt she was mostly concerned about them making a scene. Lady Frome is not one for scenes."

"I can imagine."

Katie stayed quiet, staring into her tea. It was almost as if she'd forgotten that I was sitting there.

"You seem troubled," I said.

Katie broke from her reverie and looked up at me. "I overheard the earl say he was glad that old busybody was dead. I was shocked. What a callous thing to say."

I had to stop myself from saying that I wasn't surprised. The earl? Callous? Go figure.

Katie looked around nervously and then lowered her voice again. "The earl claimed he hadn't been out with a gun at all yesterday but..." She stopped, and I held my breath, trying to be patient and let Katie speak in her own time. "But...I heard him banging the cabinets in the gun room. He came out wearing his hunting tweeds."

I felt my eyebrows shoot up. "Yesterday. You're certain? When was he in the gun room?"

"In the evening. He went out and came in again, then he

rushed upstairs. By the time the police arrived, he was wearing ordinary clothes."

"Why would he lie to the police about not using his gun that day, Katie?"

She shrugged. "It doesn't look good, I know. But the earl isn't a *murderer*. A bit cranky and self-important, yes. But deadly? No."

"That may be so, but you have to tell the police what you heard."

She rubbed her cast as though it was the arm that pained her. "I've been working for the family for decades, Poppy. The earl would never a hurt a soul. Why cause trouble?"

I swallowed. What I had to say next wouldn't be easy, but Katie needed to hear it. "I was at the murder scene yesterday," I began, thinking carefully about how to choose my words. "I was out walking with Susan Bentley, and we discovered Marlene. The cartridge from the shot that killed her was nearby. It was from the same kind of shotgun as the earl uses."

"Purdey?" she asked in a whisper.

I nodded.

The color drained from her face, and she set her teacup back in its saucer. "But that doesn't mean it was *his* gun," she whispered. "Or that he fired it." She fell silent and played with the bottom of her apron. "Look, if it turns out his gun killed that woman, then I'll come forward. But you must promise me, Poppy, not a word about what I told you."

I was disappointed, but I wouldn't break Katie Donegal's trust. I'd been trying to get her to open up to me for weeks. And now that Katie had put her confidence in me, I felt emboldened to ask the questions that had kept me awake all night. It was time to ask her what she knew about my dad. The coincidence of the song would have to wait.

"Katie, what you told me last week about Valerie leaving here because she was pregnant was so helpful. But I haven't been able to stop thinking about who my dad might be. I think you were right; he might have been one of the local lads. But I also think he disappeared from Broomewode around the same time as Valerie. Do you remember any local lads going missing?" I swallowed hard. "Or dying?"

"Dying? Why would you think that?"

"I'm nearly certain my father is dead."

Katie shook her head. Her mouth was set in a firm line. She was closing up again. Whatever moment of vulnerability we'd just shared had dissolved.

"I really haven't the foggiest who the father may have been. But I have been thinking about Valerie this week."

I leaned forward in my seat. Any information about my birth mom was gold dust. My heart was in my throat, and I could barely manage to ask, "Did you remember something else?"

She nodded. "Valerie used to talk to the old countess. Unlike the current Lady Frome, her predecessor wasn't one to disdain the company of servants. Valerie was a bright girl. I think they shared an interest in local herbs and plants."

At that I smiled. Images of Susan Bentley's herb garden flashed through my mind, of me helping her tie up the green, fragrant bundles with string.

"That makes sense," I said. "I'm sure the countess gave Valerie her shawl."

"Shawl?" Katie asked.

"The one that's in the oil painting in the dining room. The

one we tried to look at last week but had been taken 'for cleaning.'"

"It sounds like something the old countess would do. She was that generous. Valerie left here when she was pregnant. I don't know if she stayed in the area or if she left. Maybe her and the countess stayed in touch."

At this I sighed, and Katie leaned over the table and touched my hand. And then, just like she said to me last week, Katie whispered gently, "Let it be, lovey. Let it be."

"I can't. What is it you won't tell me?"

She heaved a great sigh. "Not won't, dear. Can't."

"But—"

"Trust me, nothing good can come of you asking questions." She raised her head and looked out through the kitchen window. "Especially now."

I smiled weakly and nodded. But I wouldn't let it be. I couldn't. It was the story of my birth, and I was going to find out what happened, no matter how many barriers to the truth were in my way.

I thanked Katie for her time, assured her that I would never dream of breaking her confidence in me, and then excused myself. I'd stayed far longer than I'd intended, and there was a showstopper that needed to be baked.

"Good luck, dearie," Katie said as she walked me to the door. "I'll be rooting for you today."

I stepped out into sunshine. "Thank you. I need all the well-wishes I can get."

At that, Katie crossed both sets of fingers. I waved goodbye and began my walk back to the inn. It was time to focus all my attention on *The Great British Baking Contest* and guarantee my place in the next round.

As I'd guessed, Katie knew more than she'd told me, and for the first time, she'd as good as admitted it. "Can't"? What did that even mean? And "Especially now"? Once more I ended up more frustrated leaving Broomewode Hall than I'd been when I arrived.

CHAPTER 16

*B*y the time I got back to the inn, it was almost nine a.m. Gerry was floating around in the hallway, trying to unlock the cleaning cupboard, which was tucked neatly under the stairs. He spun round as I approached him, obviously shocked that I wasn't at the tent.

"Where—" he started to ask, but I cut him off.

"Up at the hall," I explained, "trying to figure some stuff out. But I left with more questions than when I went."

Gerry wagged his finger at me. "What—"

Again, I cut him off. "I know, I know, but it's important. And I'm going to make it to the tent on time. Just one coffee. And a muffin."

Gerry opened his mouth to speak and then closed it again. I guessed by now he knew that there was no arguing with me when I was following the trail of a lead.

"If only you could use a phone." I shook my head. "You'd be the best sidekick."

Gerry stuck out his chest proudly. "I might not be able to make a phone call, but I *do* have other uses. And believe me, if I could, I'd be ringing my ex-girlfriends to give them hell, *and* my horrible old boss, and—"

I laughed. "Point taken."

He wished me luck, and I raced upstairs to drop off my cardigan and put in the same tortoise hoops and wear the same clothes I'd been wearing yesterday. Gina would have to do her magic again with the rest of my appearance—if I got there in time, that is.

Downstairs, I was expecting the breakfast room to be empty, but there was Florence, still eating breakfast. I went to the buffet table and grabbed a bacon roll, a spoonful of scrambled eggs and a hot black coffee. I wouldn't have time for anything else. I joined my friend, who was wolfing down the last mouthful of a plate of scrambled eggs and toast. As usual, she was a vision, yesterday's outfit pristine and her hair and makeup styled with her professional eye. I smoothed down my slightly crinkled shirt dress.

Florence looked at me, aghast. "Where have you been, Poppy? Have you seen the time?"

I nodded and tried to smile. "Cutting it fine, aren't we?"

"Don't tell me—you went for a walk." She didn't wait for an answer, just shook her head at me and gestured at my coffee. "If only we could mainline the java, right? I need a caffeine drip. I've no idea where to find the energy for the showstopper today."

"Tell me about it," I commiserated.

This week's showstopper theme was one I'd been looking forward to. We were to be inspired by another great British tradition, the Chelsea Flower Show. The idea was to construct and incorporate the flavors of a perfectly imagined garden, but the added kicker was that the cake had to be at least three tiers.

It had felt like the perfect topic for me, combining my love of botany and design, and I'd gone back to the sketchbook of flowers I'd filled a couple of weeks ago to illustrate a new hard-back book about the English country garden. The publisher was famous for their beautifully designed books, which show-cased the best of English heritage, and this week I'd been sent a mock-up of some of the pages where my work would feature (perfect timing or what) and had been re-inspired by what I saw. Vivid pink azaleas, their delicate petals a symbol of gentleness and femininity; sunshine-yellow freesias with their long stems graced by strange but beautiful knots of flowers; sweet multi-color pansies; pink and white tulips; tall foxgloves; the puffy, round heads of alliums, which reminded me of brightly colored cotton wool balls. In my garden, flowers didn't grow only in certain seasons, but everything bloomed year-round, so I could mix the most delicate rose buds with the richest, dusky chrysan-themums and get away with it. However, I couldn't just throw on a flower arrangement to honor the flower show theme. No, it had to have a good story and a clever flavor combination, too.

This is where my prep hit a wall. Margaret, my kitchen ghost, had been no help. She was still of the mind that gardens should be manicured to within an inch of their lives, all topiary and strict, tidy beds with flowers all lined up in a row like ladies in waiting. But I was a sucker for wild gardens where colors burst forth in surprising combinations and there was no order or sense to the planting, like a true meadow. Thing is, that wouldn't do for a cake. I didn't want to be accused of sloppy style. Somehow it had to be spontaneous and fresh-looking but also carefully designed. I'd worked all week to get the balance right, but I was going to have to stay on top of each element if I was going to complete it in time.

By the end of the week, I thought I'd come up with the unique solution to incorporating a variety of flowers into my cake. But now I had to put it to the test.

"Come on, come on," Florence said, "no time for daydreaming or dawdling either. Let's get ourselves to the tent."

I took a final bite of my bacon roll (crispy with just the right amount of ketchup), ran back to my room to brush my teeth, then let Florence drag me off to the tent, the remnants of my black coffee still languishing, undrunk, at the bottom of my cup.

As we walked, Florence told me about her showstopper. She had grand plans as usual and was making a blackberry and pear cake with an almond sponge. The fruits weren't seasonal, but it was a delicious combination. I'd worried a lot more about the decoration than the cake itself, and she'd obviously worked in the opposite direction. "I'm decorating with fresh flowers," she said. "The most beautiful white peonies you've ever seen. I spent all week looking for the perfect bloom. I'm going with a pure, white garden. I'm sure some of the bakers will throw all sorts of flowers together." She wrinkled her nose in distaste. "Gosh, isn't it hot this morning? I hope it doesn't get roasting in the tent."

Gerry appeared, running ahead of us and pretending to fan Florence with great dramatic fanfare. I had to stifle a giggle.

"What is it, Poppy?" Florence's dark eyes were wide with dismay. "Are you sick?"

"No, no," I said quickly. "I had a sudden panic I didn't have enough eggs in the tent for today, but I've got plenty, I'm sure."

"Silly goose," Florence said. "You could always borrow some of mine. Now let's pick up the pace."

I smiled as Gerry leapt ahead, bowing like an Elizabethan courtier all the way. Soon I was back in the tent, in Gina's hair and makeup chair, being thoroughly chastised for my tardiness.

She redid my hair and makeup, and then, with a final slick of lip gloss, I was good to go. "I'm cheering you on, Pops," Gina whispered.

As soon as I was miked up, I took up position behind my workstation and waited for the hosts to arrive.

Everyone looked nervous. As well we might. In a few hours' time, someone would be going home. *Don't let it be me,* I silently prayed.

The judges entered, and Arty stepped forward to introduce the segment. He cleared his throat like an officious judge about to decree their ruling. "For this week's showstopper, the bakers must produce at least a three-tiered cake which adheres to a Chelsea Flower Show theme. We're looking for floral, fruity or botanical flavors and superb decoration that will transport us into an imaginary but delicious garden."

"Heaven on earth," Jilly added. "That's what our judges are looking for."

And who wasn't?

"For this challenge, I'm renaming you The Botanical

Bakers," Arty said. "Take the energy of a rock band into your baking, guys," Arty said, erupting into a mini headbanging session, his long hair flopping over his face.

Jilly laughed. "Before Arty gets carried away with his delusional dreams of rock stardom, I think you'd better get baking! Your time starts... NOW!"

Arty smoothed his hair down and tucked the long strands behind his ears. Had they breakfasted together this morning? Something was definitely going on between them.

But now wasn't the time to ponder the mysteries of other people's romantic lives. It was showstopper time. I banished any lingering thoughts about the comedians' love lives, my birth family, the hawk, Marlene and the other bird-watchers, and the earl and his entourage of hunting fellows. One deep breath in, one big exhale, and then I started measuring my ingredients.

Arty and Jonathon went to Amara first; Elspeth and Jilly to Daniel, on the other side of the tent. I was thankful that I could begin baking in pure peace—no difficult questions from the master bakers, no jibes from the comedians.

I was making a lemon and poppy-seed cake—it was about time I got my namesake ingredient in the mix. Each tier would have a different flavor: Swiss meringue butter-cream, beginning with lemon, then raspberry, and then strawberry, then rosewater and lemon again. When they'd said at least three tiers, I took that to mean "start there." I'd decorate my creation with spun-sugar flowers, which I'd practiced making into a variety of species: pansy, rose, and sunflower, some painted with edible paint and some sprayed with edible gold. I hoped they'd add crunch and sweetness —and would be something no one else was doing. I'd chosen to stay away from real flowers, as that was the obvious route.

It was hard to keep coming up with original ideas, but I thought my garden of spun-sugar flowers was going to be fun. As usual, it was a lot to get done in time. I was going to need to summon up some concentration of the highest order.

After I'd tenderly placed my cake tins into the oven and wished them well, I took a moment to glance out at the summer landscape. As usual, we had spectators who'd come to watch the filming from behind a rope, vigilantly patrolled by Martin, of course.

My gaze rose higher, and there he was. My hawk, swooping silent and majestic far above Broomewode, looking down on us all.

"I hope I can make you proud," I whispered, as though I really were talking to my dad.

CHAPTER 17

*T*ime flowed, and I kept my head down and let the rhythm of baking take over. I loved when I could get into the flow, when my hands moved almost of their own accord.

My workstation neighbors were eerily quiet—no banter, no cheeky chat.

Elspeth was talking to Hamish, who was handling the pressure with his usual laid-back attitude. He was using some unusual ingredients, setting chamomile alongside honey and orange blossom. I thought it sounded delicious, but Elspeth was a little skeptical. "You're going to have to get the balance of those flavors spot-on," she warned. "Chamomile and orange blossom can both have a dry, tannic quality to them, even though they're subtle and fragrant. That honey could bring out the best in them both if you get it right. But too much, and it'll be sticky in texture and one-dimensional in taste."

Oh wow. Elspeth was seriously on her baking game today.

Wise words. I only hoped they would be helpful for Hamish, not a fright.

I set about making my buttercreams, and soon it was time to check on my sponges. I rushed over to the oven. They'd risen nicely and taken on a gorgeous golden color. I tried to ignore the cameras trained on my every move as I brought them back to my workstation to cool. I always worried I was going to drop my cakes. Even though that had never happened in my life, there could always be a first—and I didn't want that to happen with an audience of a million people, thanks.

Now for the spun-sugar flowers. This was the trickiest part. I'd have to work quickly. I dissolved my sugar in boiling water and left it to bubble away until it turned pale caramel in color. I had to be careful not to let it crystalize. I turned off the heat and then gently poured the mixture across the handles of a row of wooden spoons so that it would harden in strands and I could turn them into flower shapes. It was fiddly work, and my heart was in my mouth the whole time, praying that I wouldn't snap the delicate sugar strands.

The whole process was taking much longer than it had while I was practicing. I was beginning to stress out, so I stopped what I was doing and closed my eyes for a moment. I tried to channel Elspeth's calming voice. *Calm down, Poppy. One step at a time. If you can't make ten, then aim for six or seven.*

But as I kept working with the cooling sugar, I realized that I'd begun to perspire. Not just at the temples in nervousness but from the heat. I looked around me and saw that every contestant, as well as the hosts, was flushed, waving their hands about, trying to cool their cheeks.

"Is it just me, or is the temperature in here rising?" I said to Florence.

"It's boiling!" she said. "I can feel my foundation slipping down my cheeks. And if that's happening to me, think about what it's going to do to our icing."

"Oh, man," I said. "You're right. We're going to have to work super fast if they're going to set."

With my sponge cool, it was time to stack my tiers. I'd have to abandon the idea of making more sugar flowers. I put them to the side and then piped a round of buttercream onto my board and placed the first sponge on top. I spooned a thin layer of buttercream on top of the sponge and spread it evenly to the edges and then did the same with the other tiers.

Now for the bit I had most trouble with. I piped buttercream around the cake, starting on the top and working my way down the sides, using a palette knife to smooth it out as I went. I wanted each inch to be covered, but the heat in the tent was making things difficult. To my horror, the buttercream started to slide. I worked double-quick and then took the cake to chill in the fridge and firm up before I added another layer of buttercream.

I still had to pipe the flowers that would mix with my spun-sugar blooms. I began to think I'd been too ambitious.

"Twenty minutes to go, bakers," Jilly called out.

I gulped. Would I have enough time to set my second layer of buttercream? Well, I had no choice—I'd have to make it work.

I administered the second layer of buttercream, put it back in the chiller, and sprayed my sugar flowers gold. With five minutes to go, I assembled the lot, trying to create a wild garden effect with my sugar blooms mixed with my piped roses and daisies. But I'd underestimated how many flowers I'd have time for. The five-tiered cake was enormous and a bit lacking in blooms. It was more community garden than Chelsea Flower Show.

But there was no time to make any more. Arty announced that our time was up. I took my cake over to the judging table, hoping that its taste would make up for its lack of show-stopper appeal.

First up was Daniel. He looked hot and worried, and his cake did, too.

"This cake is all over the place," Jonathon said. "The décor's not great." He sliced into it and shook his head. "It's soggy." He prodded at the slice.

"I'm afraid, Daniel, that your cake isn't quite cooked through." Elspeth turned the tray to the side so that the camera could zoom in on Daniel's mistake. Inwardly, I cringed for him. An underdone cake was an easy thing to slip up on—I'd done the same countless times during practice runs.

Daniel wiped at a bead of sweat. "It needed longer, I know. I ran out of time."

Next up was Maggie. We all knew that Elspeth wasn't a great admirer of rose as an ingredient. "To grow and admire, not to taste" was her catchphrase. So Maggie had taken a big risk with her strawberry, vanilla, and rose number. But there was no denying it—the three-tiered cake was an out and out beauty. The sponge itself was simple enough, vanilla filled with fresh strawberry buttercream that also generously coated the outside of the cake. But it was the piped roses that stole the show. Each layer of the cake was crowned by a ring of rose-flavored blooms, red for the bottom, pink for the middle, and white at the top. It was breathtaking.

"Now this is a beauty," Jonathon said, gazing at the cake. "How you managed to do all this fine piping work in the time is a marvel."

"I have to agree," Elspeth said. "This is something quite special. But as always, it has to taste as good as it looks."

We watched as they cut into the top tier and removed a slice of cake. It looked perfect. A lovely crumb, smooth-looking buttercream, a wedge of delicate rose. I patted Maggie on the shoulder. "Amazing," I mouthed. She glowed with pleasure.

And I wasn't the only one who thought so. "This is wonderful. Truly, Maggie. What a marvel. I was worried about that rose flavor—you know it's not my favorite—but here it really works with the creamy vanilla. A triumph."

Next up was Amara, who was looking very worried indeed. As well she might—who'd want to follow Maggie after that kind of praise?

I knew Amara had been struggling this weekend. Her four tiers were decorated with hydrangeas and roses piped in buttercream, but haste and heat had worked against her.

"Your flowers are wilted, Amara," Jonathon said, stating the obvious.

"It's a bit of a mess," Elspeth agreed.

Amara nodded, looking frazzled. The judging never got any easier. My heart went out to her. As they tried her cake, I realized I was nervously fiddling with my earrings and dropped my hands back to my sides, again.

Jonathon looked to Elspeth, who said, "The flavors are so subtle, I can't distinguish them at all."

Amara hung her head.

"Elderflower is always a tricky ingredient," Jonathon added, looking to Elspeth as if for approval.

Elspeth nodded. "It likes to play hide and seek with other ingredients. Very good at hiding, not so good at seeking."

They moved onto Gaurav's creation. It was a work of art. He'd gone with a Garden of Eden theme, and there was an apple tree with a green snake coiled along the bottom.

"Ten out of ten for creative flair," Jonathon announced, turning the board to see the cake from all angles. "You've told a story with your decorations. It's certainly not easy to do that within your allotted time, so I'm impressed with this."

"It's cinnamon and apple, is that right?" Elspeth asked.

Gaurav said yes, explaining that he'd also added some succulent sultanas on a last-minute whim.

"Well, it works!" Elspeth said. "This is a sumptuous, moist cake with delightful flavors. Just goes to show that the briefs can be interpreted in many ways. It can pay to think outside the box."

Go, Gaurav, I thought. He was really bringing it to the competition this week.

Florence came next, and the judges praised her creation, too. To go along with her fresh flowers, she'd created some gorgeous foliage out of fondant. When Elspeth said the cake had a professional finish, Florence beamed.

And then it was my turn. It seemed cruel to judge Florence and me side by side again, but there you go. I tried not to wince as Jonathon and Elspeth appraised my bake.

"The golden sugar flowers are a delight," Elspeth said, "but your piped flowers are a little clumsy."

I nodded my head in agreement. She was right.

Jonathon sliced the cake, and they each tried a forkful from the lemon buttercream tier and the raspberry one.

"The flavors are great," Jonathon said. "Raspberry and lemon are a good combination; the poppy seed adds an interesting texture to the sponge. I just would have liked a bit more ambition with this. It's not as much of a showstopper as you've shown yourself to be capable of."

Elspeth nodded. "This is a good bake. The crumb is perfect, the filling rich and satisfying. But perhaps something like a lemon curd sandwiched between the layers might have added some oomph. Having the same buttercream as the outside might have been a mistake. But overall, this is a good cake and very tasty."

I let out my breath. Okay. That could have been worse. But it wasn't the glowing review I'd hoped for.

The judges left to confer, and when they returned, it was no surprise that they named Maggie the winner of this round. Florence was second and Gaurav third, which meant I was in the middle of the pack again with Hamish this time. Amara and Daniel were at the bottom.

It was time for the star baker to be announced. As well as the name of the person going home today. I held my breath. I knew that my name definitely wouldn't be called out for star baker. But would this be the day I said goodbye to the show?

No surprises, the judges chose Florence as this week's star baker. She'd had a blinding weekend, and I was proud of her.

"Sadly, it falls to me to bid farewell to one of our contestants," Jilly said.

The mood changed instantly. Everyone stiffened, bracing themselves for bad news.

"This has been a really tough weekend."

Amara nodded. She looked so anxious, my heart went out to her.

"The contestant going home today is a brilliant baker. We've really enjoyed having them on the show. But I'm afraid that, Daniel, this is the end of the road for you. We'll miss you, our dentist with the sweet tooth."

Oh, poor Daniel. He'd really struggled this week, but I was also surprised that Amara had made it through. I had a feeling it could have gone either way. And then there I was, Average Poppy, not too shabby but not shining, either.

Daniel hugged us all and accepted the usual compliments and backslappings.

When Elspeth and Jonathon said nice things to him, he replied, "This has been an amazing roller coaster," he said. "I've learned so much about myself being on this show. I know now that although dentistry is my practice and also my passion, baking is giving it a run for its money. I'm going to leave the show with more ambition than I started with. I know now how to be more accurate in my measurements, how to balance ingredients using the science behind how they interact. I'm going to keep going. And hopefully become a better baker."

It was a beautiful speech, and when it was my turn to hug him and wish him well, he said, "I'm gutted, obviously, but I can't wait to spend the weekends with my wife and kids again. A kitchen isn't a kitchen without my family in it."

And now that I was safe for another week, I could get back on the trail of finding out who my birth dad was. I'd also like to help get justice for Marlene. And I was going to need all the help that I could get. Starting with Mitty, the gamekeeper's father.

CHAPTER 18

*A*fter a long, hot day of baking, we arrived back at the pub a giggly, exhausted, relieved group. I tried to be patient with Florence as she told stories, holding court as the cake queen for the weekend. But as I listened, getting hold of the old gamekeeper was the only thing on my mind. Mitty was my best chance of getting some answers about Marlene and maybe even my dad. I was champing at the bit to get on the trail and see where it led me.

Hamish grabbed our usual table, and everyone half-collapsed into the seats, exhausted. Everyone, that is, but me. After I'd secured a place in the competition next week, a sudden wave of energy had engulfed me. Maybe it was Daniel's heartfelt speech, or perhaps something more mysterious was at play. Either way, my vigor was renewed, and I felt compelled to get on the case of Marlene's murder. And solve it—no matter what, or who, I might come up against in the process. Justice had to be served.

"First round's on me," Daniel said.

I asked for lemonade, as I needed my wits about me. After chatting with the group for a few minutes, I slipped away to the bar, where Eve was polishing glasses.

"Any luck?" I asked. But her expression said it all.

"Sorry, Poppy. After you asked this morning, I called every single care home between here and Chippenham. Mitty isn't registered at any of them. Maybe you got the name of the town wrong? Is it important?"

I wondered if Katie had mixed up the town names, or could she have *purposely* told me the wrong place? Was there something she didn't want me to find out? Katie had certainly proved herself to be slippery before. I didn't want to waste time on a dead lead.

"I don't know. Marlene said she was going to visit Mitty the day she was killed. She was such an energetic woman, I thought she might have seen him that very day. I want to speak to him, see if she was acting strangely or confided anything in him. Any small clue could help." I also wanted to ask about my father, but I didn't share that with Eve. I didn't want another warning to forget the past.

Eve gave me a serious look. "It's an honorable thing to go after Marlene's murderer, but please be careful, Poppy. Arthur isn't exactly a prince among men. He's not going to like you poking around in his family business. Tell the police what you know."

I lowered my voice. "I feel like maybe it's my fault she died."

"Why on earth would you think that?" Eve looked shocked.

"Because we willed protection for the wild birds without

thinking how it would be accomplished. What if it's our spell that drew Marlene and her group here to protest?"

"Even so, our magic doesn't harm."

"No. But our magic could have put that woman in harm's path."

She shook her head. "You've much to learn yet, my dear." She might have said more, but Florence came up to ask for water. "Have to stay hydrated," she reminded me. "You want your skin to look fresh on camera."

I looked over at where the rest of the bakers were popping a bottle of prosecco. They were so merry, flushed with happiness—even Daniel, who was excited to go home and see his family. I wanted to join them, to let myself revel in the relief of another weekend over, my position in the competition secure. But I didn't feel like I had the luxury of resting—not yet. I knew of two people who would definitely know where Mitty lived. The earl and Arthur. Of the two of them, I'd rather confront the gamekeeper than the gun-happy earl.

When Florence took the water to the table, I told Eve that I'd be back soon and then slipped away. With any luck, I'd be back before the rest of the bakers left.

I raced up the stairs for a quick shower and changed into jeans, a T-shirt and sneakers, then rushed out through the back door and onto the path that would take me to the gamekeeper's cottage. I wasn't going to be a welcome visitor, that was for sure, but I needed Arthur to tell me where his father was.

I could tell Arthur the truth, that I was hoping his father might remember mine. If I asked a few questions about Marlene, that was between me and Mitty.

I knew the police were investigating the earl in Marlene's death. Whether he'd simply lost his temper with her protests about the land and hunting laws or he'd shot her by accident, all the clues led back to the earl. He and Marlene had argued the day before she died. The cartridge used in his Purdey shotgun had been found, and it was a heavy load—almost two ounces when only an ounce was needed for birds. And then there was Katie Donegal's confession. She'd seen the earl go out with his gun, wearing his hunting tweeds, around the time Marlene was killed.

Most suspiciously, he'd changed clothes before the police arrived and lied when they questioned him.

As I walked, I relived the last time I'd gone this way.

I stopped in my tracks, recalling the moment I'd met up with Susan Bentley. She was walking Sly, which she did frequently, but could she have had some reason to wish Marlene harm?

I couldn't imagine why, but if I'd learned anything recently, it was that murder had a murky past, born in secrets, old wounds and unexpressed anger. Was there more to Susan's dog walk than I'd realized?

Martin, the security guard, roused my suspicions, too. He was never where he was supposed to be, leaving his post by the tent to wander the grounds, and he'd handled Marlene with an unnecessary brusqueness. We'd bumped into him wandering around on the night of the murder. What had he been doing there?

But even still, the evidence pointing at the earl was compelling.

There was part of me that felt bad for Benedict. He'd been so quick to defend his dad—about his hunting regime, about the type and weight of the shotgun's cartridge. *Of course* he didn't want to believe that his dad was capable of murder. Who would? But I had a gut-deep instinct that the earl would stoop to any treachery for his own benefit.

Before long, the gamekeeper's cottage came into view. I stopped for a moment and looked round, half expecting to see Marlene's restless spirit wandering about the place, brandishing her binoculars, searching for the earl to give him a piece of her mind. If the image hadn't been so tragic, I would have smiled—Marlene had enough spirit for this world and the next one put together.

But Marlene didn't appear. She'd made it safely over to the other side. I was glad—she didn't deserve to be stuck. No, what she deserved was justice.

I headed straight for the cottage, determined to find out how I could reach Mitty.

It was my third visit to the cottage, and like the first time, when I'd accidentally stumbled across the building trying to stay out of the earl's way, I heard muffled noises coming from inside. It was still too bright outside for any lights to be on, but I figured the sound was the TV again, blaring even louder than it was before. Arthur really needed to have his ears checked.

I stepped off the path onto the springy green lawn and walked up the stone path to the front door. There was no doorbell, just a brass knocker. I took a deep breath and then rapped the door three times. I waited. And then I waited some more. Nothing. The sound of the TV was deafening, even from outside. Maybe the gamekeeper had ruined his hearing from all that shooting. I didn't feel very sympathetic.

I tried knocking again, harder this time. I waited another

full minute and then began to worry. What if whoever had killed Marlene had it in for the gamekeeper too? Could Arthur be lying in that cottage, hurt?

I went around the side of the cottage, hoping to peer in through a window or find the back door unlocked. I touched my purple amethyst necklace and quickly recited a protection spell, feeling a chill even in the afternoon sun.

I returned to the side window I'd found on Friday, but the thick white netting was still drawn, blocking any view of inside. I tried knocking on the window, too, in the hope that maybe I'd be heard from here. But again—nothing.

I moved to the back, where the baby grouse wandered freely in the sunshine. They were so sweet. I wished I could take all of them home with me and let them live a happy life far away from the world of shotguns. But now so wasn't the time to plan a bird farm. I turned the handle to the back door, heart in mouth, half afraid of walking into Arthur's kitchen, where he might be in trouble. Or cooking naked. Ugh.

It couldn't be coincidence that the spell I'd most recently learned was an unlocking one. After a week or so of practicing opening my own kitchen door with my powers, it was time to put my new skill to good use.

I closed my eyes and concentrated on the sound of the TV coming from inside. But as well as the indistinct chatter of daytime TV, I found myself tuning in to another sound. I couldn't pinpoint what it was exactly. Maybe it was more of an energy than a sound, but it was a desperate energy. A sense of unease, of unrest. It was the same feeling I got when I came across unhappy spirits. Distress. Acute distress. My eyes snapped back open. I shuddered. Something was seriously wrong in there. I didn't like Arthur, but if I could help him, I would.

I closed my eyes again and tried to train my thoughts on opening the door. It was an old, heavy-looking oak door. Much thicker than any I'd tried to open before. Worse, the lock was much newer and pretty heavy-duty.

Knowing someone inside was in trouble, I had to concentrate and not doubt myself. Silently, I called on my power and the deep, magic energy that drew so many witches to this area. Slowly, I recited:

> *Earth, water, fire and air,*
> *Help me to get from here to there.*
> *Open this lock; let my wish be the key.*
> *As I will, so mote it be.*

The familiar energy surge began to rush through me, starting in the tips of my toes and working its way up and up until my hands felt as though they were buzzing with electricity. I turned my wrist, pictured myself turning a key in a lock, and then I opened my eyes. The door handle began to turn slowly, so slowly, but I kept my concentration locked, focusing everything I had on an image of the door opening.

Finally, it swung open.

I dropped my hands to my knees, trying to get my breath back and slow my racing heart. The energy rushed out of me, and I felt as depleted as if I'd just run a marathon (or how I'd imagine running a marathon felt).

I filled my lungs, breathing in and out, in and out, until I felt strong enough to walk through that open door.

I crossed the threshold, and just as I imagined, I walked straight into the kitchen. It was messy—dirty bowls and plates stacked in a haphazard pile by the sink. Toast crumbs on the countertop. But the room was empty.

I followed the sound of the TV, exiting the kitchen and walking along a dim hallway. On the walls hung a series of oil portraits, similar in style to those I'd seen at Broomewode Hall. For a moment, I felt certain I'd find the portrait of the old countess and my baby blanket, but my mind was playing games with me. The portraits were all of men with similar features, Arthur's grandfather and great-grandfather, I assumed, and one of a horse.

I passed an empty living room, a dining room that looked dusty and unused. A pile of magazines and what looked like bills covered the surface of the old table.

The sound of the TV grew and grew, and I followed its terrible blare until I reached a door that I figured opened out onto the side room whose window had been blocked with netting. My heart beat double time.

The feeling of distress I'd sensed outside grew. Someone was in there.

I steeled myself and then turned the door handle. Argh, not again. It was locked.

I stared at the closed door. My energy was so low, would I be able to use magic to open another lock? *You've got no choice,* I told myself. *Someone's in trouble. Give it everything you've got left.*

I closed my eyes, and this time the power surge came much quicker, almost overtaking me. I began to feel wobbly, like I couldn't control my own body. *Stay strong, Pops. Stay strong.* I swallowed hard and visualized the door unlocking. I stood that way, body shaking, hands fizzing with electricity for what seemed eons. And then I heard a click.

For such a small sound, it had a big impact on me. I nearly jumped for joy. I was getting good at this stuff.

The door was ajar. A door that had previously been locked. But I guessed they hadn't figured on taking on a witch.

Slowly, I edged towards the open door, afraid of what I would find inside.

The sound of the TV was terrible, another soap opera, Australian this time, the actors embroiled in some kind of dispute.

I tiptoed inside and almost gagged on the smell. The darkened room was oppressive, stifling, the atmosphere heavy with decay. I clapped my hand over my mouth. A thick layer of dust coated the air. I squinted and saw an old TV in one corner, its flashing colors casting strange shadows on the floor.

And that's when I saw him: an old man in a rumpled half-made bed, his shoulders and head propped up against a dark headboard. He was wearing a stained brown dressing gown, open at the neck, and the grease of his gray hair, swept back at odd angles from his temples, caught the light of the TV. His cheeks were stubbled and hollow, and there was a small cut on his chin. He stared at me in mute horror. And then I realized I'd seen that face before. The very first time I'd met Arthur, an image of him as a father, playing with a young child, suddenly popped into my brain. The vision surprised me, as Arthur was brandishing a shotgun at the time, and I'd wondered why such a tender scene had come to me. But now I could see that I'd been wrong. The image wasn't of Arthur as a father, playing with his son. It was *Arthur's* father.

"Mitty?" I whispered.

CHAPTER 19

"*M*itty?" I repeated. "Is that you?"

The old man opened his mouth, but no words came out.

"Mitty," I whispered. "It *is* you. Can you move?"

The man shook his head ever so slightly. He looked to be in pain.

"I'm going to get help. Right now. Don't you worry. Let's get you out of here."

I ran down the corridor and out through the back door. But I hadn't thought it through—who was I running to? The nearest building was Broomewode Hall, and I wasn't about to run straight into the arms of a murderer.

I reached for my cell phone and then remembered I'd plugged it in to recharge. I couldn't believe I'd been so brainless.

What to do?

This wasn't an emergency that required an ambulance. I felt I needed to get some advice and local support. This was going to require some delicacy.

Susan Bentley was also closer than the inn. I could get her advice. She knew the area better than I did and hopefully would know the right person or organization to call. Besides, two witches were better than one.

I picked up my pace, turning onto the path that led to the farm. But suddenly I heard a man calling my name. Had the help come to me? I stopped and spun around. But what I saw sent shivers of fear through me. It was Arthur. And in his arms was a shotgun pointed straight at me.

I was frozen to the spot.

"Stop right there, missy. Think you can break into my property and then just run off?"

I held up my hands in a sign of surrender, and he laughed. "There are laws against trespass, you know. You're as bad as those twitchers. Think you're above the law?"

Even though I was terrified—having a shotgun pointed at your heart will do that—I was too furious to be sensible. "It's against the law to keep your poor father locked up and sitting in his own filth. How could you do that?"

Arthur's face dropped, and his features twisted. It was the first time I'd seen him without a flat cap on, and his tufts of pale brown hair were sticking out at angles. All the softness around his brown eyes had disappeared, and I could see now that the sloping shoulders that I'd first thought had made him appear humble were actually the stance of someone hiding something, their body caving in under the weight of a secret. A terrible, dark secret.

Arthur still hadn't shifted his aim, and I was staring down the barrel of a shotgun. He took a step closer. Talk about toying with a beast. I was beginning to regret my outburst.

Come on. Think. What could I do to walk away from this?

Surrender and plead with him? Or make a run for it? I'd seen Arthur hunting, and I didn't fancy my chances against his aim. I didn't know what to do. I didn't think he did, either. No doubt he was trying to work out what to do with my body if he killed me.

The cry of a hawk echoed through the sky. I looked up. It was *my* hawk. Even as I felt its power joining mine, Arthur began to curse the bird and angled his gun away from me and up to the sky.

"NO!" I screamed.

The hawk circled wildly, still screeching a high-pitched warning sound. His beautiful wings were stretched to their greatest span, the chestnut feathers fading into white, tail jutting out. His legs were poised, ready to attack, black talons glinting in the sun.

"Why did you kill Marlene?" I shouted, trying to bring Arthur's attention away from the hawk and back to me. "I know it was YOU."

He lowered the gun so it was once more pointing at me.

I knew I had to stay steady and firm. *Don't lose your cool now, Pops.* I swallowed and in as level a voice as I could manage, considering a gun was pointing at me, said, "I just can't figure out why. Did Marlene find out that you're keeping your poor father locked in a room? Have you been pocketing the money the Champneys have been paying for him to live in an expensive home?"

As I spoke, I tried to concentrate my energy on the shotgun. Surely if I focused enough, I could move the weapon? But I couldn't summon the energy. Was I depleted from my double door-opening trick earlier? On top of that marathon of baking today?

But as my words sank in, an expression of bitterness spread over Arthur's face. "Judge all you want, but I needed that money," Arthur admitted. "I got into debt starting my own company: The Great British Game Bird Hunt. I saw all the money the earl was making off a baking show." He shook his head as though he couldn't believe it. "Contests over cakes and pies."

"It's not as easy as you make it sound." And I had the sore back and feet to prove it.

"I was going to put on game-hunting holidays, starting here in Somerset and then expanding across the whole country—Yorkshire, the Orkneys, you name it. Guests could come for the day or long weekends, and everything would be perfectly arranged for them. I'd set up trainings, the shotguns and cartridges, have a driver chauffeur them around, and then they could stay at the inn. I was even going to get the pub to cook the game we shot. I had the whole thing worked out. I'm not going to be the earl's gamekeeper for the rest of my life. I've got ambition."

"What happened?" Because from his outraged demeanor, it was pretty clear something had gone wrong.

"Name it. I ordered the latest shotguns from a specialist supplier abroad, cost a packet they did. But they got stuck at customs. Didn't pass some stupid import law. and they held onto my guns and said they were going to prosecute. All of a sudden, I had the law coming after me. And the legal fees to sort the whole sorry mess drained every penny I had."

He stopped to get his breath.

Oh, cry me a river.

"And I spent money on an advertising firm who charged

me an arm and a leg, then said there was no market. Thieving swine."

"You're stealing the money meant to keep your father in comfort."

"You don't understand!" He was so mad, spittle was gathering in the corners of his mouth. "You didn't grow up in Broomewode, always in the shadow of your father. *Oh, good ol' Mitty. Isn't Mitty a fine fellow. Best gamekeeper we've ever had. Hope you'll turn out to be half the man.*" He spat on the ground in disdain. "Like he was a bloody saint."

I shook my head. "So you stole his hard-earned pension money, pulled him out of a good home, and let him rot in a stinky room."

"My pa doesn't know where he is anyway, so what's the difference? I take him meals three times a day. He's got the telly. We were getting on just fine until that old biddy came nosing around the cottage. Demanded to know where he was. She'd tried calling his old care home, and they told her he hadn't lived there for months, that I'd taken him away. Marlene was always sticking her nose in where it wasn't wanted. Said she was going to the earl."

Oh, Marlene.

"I told her I'd moved him to another home a bit farther away, and she demanded to know where it was. I told her to mind her own business, and she started banging on all the windows. Like she knew he was inside. I tried to stop her by talking reasonably. But she wouldn't listen."

He stopped, wiped his brow, and then straightened again and looked straight at me. "She was going to cause trouble. She was like all the vermin who come on the estate. We get rid of 'em."

I shook my head. If anyone was the vermin, it was Arthur. "But you didn't use your own gun, did you?" I said.

At this, Arthur pulled himself up to his full height. "I'm not stupid," he spat. "I didn't want this thing traced back to me. So I used what I had on hand."

"And that was the earl's shotgun."

Arthur raised one eyebrow. "Aren't you a clever little baker? It's one of them. Had the day's guns in my cottage, ready to clean. When Marlene started hollering and yelling outside the door, I grabbed the earl's shotgun."

He laughed, and the sound caused my body to seize up in fear. "I'm a much better shot than he is. I never miss." I sensed the hawk was hovering but kept my gaze steady on Arthur, who took a step toward me. "Now, we're going to take a little walk, you and I."

"So, you can shoot me and hide my body?"

"I don't have time for this. I've Pa's dinner to do."

The hawk screeched and swooped down, his talons aiming straight for Arthur's exposed head. But Arthur didn't seem in the least bit worried. In slow motion, I watched as Arthur pulled the gun snug into his shoulder and aimed it straight at me, one finger moving to hover over the trigger.

I was frozen to the spot.

"Goodbye, vermin," he said.

Time slowed. I could hear the hawk screech, but I'd be dead before it landed. I shut my eyes. *Crack crack crack.* The shotgun went off.

I waited for the burst of pain, for death. But wait, I was still here. I opened my eyes, and there was Arthur in a crumpled heap on the grass.

"Agh," he cried, grabbing at his butt.

What on earth? What just happened?

"Poppy. You all right?"

Benedict! He was holding a shotgun and ran forward, kicking the gamekeeper's gun out of reach.

I shook my head in disbelief. "You shot him?"

"In the backside. He'll be well enough to stand trial for attempted murder."

Benedict came towards me, his face softened by concern. "Are you okay?" he asked gently.

I looked at his shotgun, still stunned. "I thought you hated guns."

Benedict looked surprised. "I do hate them. But I still know how to shoot."

"Thank you," I said quietly, looking into his eyes. They were a soft brown color, gentle and full of concern. "You saved my life."

The gamekeeper was groaning and cursing.

"Blast, I haven't got my mobile on me. Have you?"

But of course, I'd left mine back at the inn.

"Hello, hello? Everyone okay?"

Benedict and I turned at the same time. It was Martin, the security guard, out on the prowl. I'd managed to bump into him twice this weekend, but where was he when some serious security was actually needed?

Martin looked amazed. "I heard shooting." He stopped. "Is he?"

"Very much alive," Benedict replied. "And very much the man who just tried to shoot Poppy."

"*And* the man who murdered Marlene," I added.

Benedict spun back to me. "He is?"

I nodded grimly. "I'll tell you everything after this maniac has been arrested. And we need to call a doctor."

"I need an ambulance," Arthur groaned.

"Not for you. For your dad." I turned to Benedict once more. "Mitty has been locked up at the gamekeeper's cottage, and he looks bad."

"That's terrible," Benedict said. Addressing Martin, Benedict's haughty voice returned, "Perhaps you could do something useful for a change and call the police." He glanced at the man writhing on the ground. "And an ambulance."

Martin's eyes lit up. "Of course, of course." He began to pat down his many pockets, looking for a phone.

Benedict rolled his eyes and, despite everything, I let out a snort of inappropriate laughter. Stress, no doubt.

"Truth is, I want to join the police, but all I've been able to get is security work," Martin said, dialing 999. "I can't wait to speak to a real detective."

So that explained why Martin was always prowling around Broomewode, too far from the baking tent to actually be of any use. And it must be why he really got into it with Marlene, too. He just wanted to assert his authority. Show that he had it in him to enforce the law.

"Tell me what happened," Benedict asked. "Mitty was like a second father to me. He's the one who taught me to shoot."

And thank you, Mitty.

"Turns out that Arthur here got himself into some financial trouble and took his father out of the expensive home your family have been paying for and pocketed the cash himself."

"You're joking."

"I wish. I was with Marlene the day she died. We were

chatting in the pub, and she got talking about Mitty—how Arthur wasn't half the man his father was. She left the pub wanting to visit her old friend. And then the next thing you know, she's dead. I found out which town Mitty had moved to but not the name of the home. I wanted to pay him a visit, see what he and Marlene talked about before she died. But Mitty wasn't in a home. I had Eve call round them while I was baking this morning. Nothing. No one by that name was registered. So I headed to the cottage to get some answers from Arthur. And that's when I found Mitty."

"The cheek of it. My parents have been paying through the teeth for that home."

"It was awful, Benedict. He was locked in a room with the TV blaring and all the curtains closed so no one would know that he was there. It smelled terrible, that unwashed fetid smell. Arthur was taking him food, but that was the extent of the care."

"I can't believe it," Benedict said sadly.

"I think Arthur felt like he could never be the man his father was. He had dreams of setting up his own hunting business, but it went wrong. He lost all his money."

"The police and the ambulance are on their way," Martin announced. "I'll wait for the detectives here. Sir, could you help escort the paramedics to the cottage? It can be hard to find."

Benedict nodded and then turned to me. "Will you head back to the inn? I don't want anything else happening to you."

I looked up at the sky and saw the hawk circling. "I have a feeling I'll be safe now."

CHAPTER 20

"*W*here have you been?" Hamish cried as I walked back into the pub.

The whole group stopped talking and stared. I didn't want this attention. I just wanted a hot bath and to forget about the events of the last few hours. But now that everyone was looking at me, I'd have to explain where I'd just disappeared off to. Again.

To my surprise, Florence came to my rescue. "Let the poor girl sit down first," she said, patting the space on the bench next to her. "Scooch, scooch. Poppy looks like she could do with a drink."

I obeyed Florence, grateful for her kindness, and accepted the glass of prosecco. I let myself enjoy the crisp bubbles.

"I'll fill you in on our gossip first," she said with authority. "And then you can spill the beans on whatever you've been up to."

I nodded, half afraid of what her gossip might be. I hoped it was something nice, like Gaurav had another date.

"Our dear friend Amara is leaving us," Florence announced with a flourish.

"What?" I said. "But Daniel was voted out."

"I know," Amara said quietly. "But I had a call from my husband a few minutes ago. My mother is ill. I'll have to fly back to India to look after her. I don't want any other doctor having control over her care. I've already spoken to the producers. I will miss you all."

I felt my mouth drop open. "I'm so sorry. I hope she'll be better soon."

"Thank you, Poppy." She sighed. "I was only waiting for you so I could say goodbye. I must be off."

And now, with two people leaving, the competition was going to be harder than ever.

"I'm so sad to see you go," I said. "You're a wonderful baker."

She stood, and we all hugged her, and then she headed out of the inn, dragging her weekender bag behind her.

Florence swiveled in my direction and told me that I wasn't off the hook yet.

I swallowed another sip—okay, it was a gulp—of prosecco and told the group what had happened at the gamekeeper's cottage, keeping my description as brief as I could. I didn't want to permanently sour the mood. This evening should be about celebration.

Everyone was silent as I recounted my run-in with Arthur. I left out the details of Mitty's sad room. No one needed to hear that sorry tale.

As my story came to a close, Edward, the gardener, came into the pub. He waved at me, and I gestured that he should join us. Florence immediately perked up and tossed her hair over her shoulders. "Sorry, Flo," I whispered. "He's been spending time with Lauren, the bride-to-be who was here last week."

"Hmph," Florence muttered. "So she ensnared him good and proper. Fair play to her, fair play."

Edward pulled up a seat. "I've just come from the manor house," he said. "What a day you've had."

I nodded grimly. What could I say? It had been awful, and I was glad to see the back of Arthur. Or, more accurately, his crumpled form, clutching his butt in pain. I still couldn't get over Benedict saving me like that. But if I'd learned anything over the past few weeks, it was that *anything* was possible. People and ghosts were full of surprises. We never stopped growing.

"They've taken Mitty to the hospital to be checked over, but the paramedics said he looked in good shape, considering," Edward said. "I thought you'd want to know."

"What a relief," I said, thanking Edward for coming to tell me.

"Arthur was taken to the hospital, too, but in handcuffs." Edward shook his head. "I hope they lock Arthur up and throw away the key. No one should treat their father that way. Benedict's talked the earl into giving Mitty one of the smaller cottages when the hospital releases him, and Katie Donegal will do the cooking for him until he's well enough to decide where he wants to go. Or perhaps he'll stay at Broomewode. It was his home for all of his life, after all."

"Good." I remembered how sure I'd been that the earl had murdered Marlene and had a flash of embarrassment. But he had acted suspiciously.

"At least we're shot of Arthur." Edward paused and looked at me. "Sorry, poor word choice. He won't be back in Broomewode for a very long time. And Arthur's son wants nothing to do with Broomewode *or* the job, especially now his dad's a killer."

"I guess there's a job opening then," I said. "Whoever takes the role, I hope they respect the land and its wildlife more."

At this, Hamish nodded passionately. "The land here is ancient, and it needs local knowledge and a good heart to take care of it properly."

Edward grinned. "I was hoping my good heart might be worthy."

Hamish raised his glass. "I think you'd be a grand gamekeeper."

I agreed. "And that way you can keep an eye on the hawk for me. He came to my rescue today, you know. They're very intelligent creatures."

He looked perturbed, then said, "I've made the earl promise he won't go out at night anymore trying to kill night hunting predators."

"I'm very happy to hear it." That must be why he'd been acting so suspicious. He hadn't murdered Marlene, but he'd been breaking the law in a different way. I was delighted Edward was making him stop his illegal hunting, and very much hoped he'd be a much better gamekeeper than his predecessor.

Maggie, Daniel and Florence said they'd have to be going, and there was a tearful farewell as we said goodbye and good luck.

In the middle of the hugs and well-wishes, Benedict

appeared and stood at the bar. I detached myself from an embrace with Maggie, telling her to enjoy her week and that I'd see her next weekend, and approached the bar.

"How are you feeling, Poppy? I was worried, but you look absolutely fine, of course. You seem to take everything in your stride."

I laughed. "It might look that way, but there's a lot going on under the surface."

Yeah, like witchcraft and mysterious birth parents and a few ghosts...

"Like a swan," Benedict said, smiling.

"Exactly," I said, thinking of the serene creatures who glided across the lake at Broomewode Hall. "But perhaps less graceful."

"Well, you certainly handled having a gun pointed at you gracefully."

"About that," I said. "I owe you a thank-you. A proper one. For saving my life. Who knows what might have happened if you hadn't come along?"

Benedict shrugged as if it was nothing, but he flushed with pleasure, and his brown eyes sparkled. "I feel that the two of us may have got off on the wrong foot. Do you think we could be friends?"

I was so shocked by Benedict's earnest question that I almost burst out laughing. Luckily, I gathered myself quickly and stuck out my hand. "I think any man who saves my life is definitely on my friends' list."

Benedict grinned and shook my hand. "Friends," he said.

"Friends."

For the first time all day, I smiled wholeheartedly.

Thank you for reading *Blood, Sweat and Tiers!* I hope you enjoyed it. Poppy's adventures in competition baking, and murder, continue in *Crumbs and Misdemeanors.* Read a sneak peek below, as the mayhem continues during bread week...

Crumbs and Misdemeanors, Chapter 1

BREAD HAD NEVER BEEN my jam, so to speak. Every baker will tell you that there is one type of bake they struggle with—it might be patisserie, biscuits, or getting a fluffy and light genoise. For me, it was bread. I don't know why I had such a tough time with that seemingly oh so simple staple. It eluded me. Was I being punished by the gluten gods for having a wickedly sweet tooth? The closer we got to bread week, the more my bread wouldn't perform. Either it didn't rise properly, or it was too dry, too wet, too heavy, or the crust was hard.

I practiced and practiced—everything from caraway seed loaf to sourdough, although I was pretty sure that the judges wouldn't demand a sourdough loaf, as it took too long. But still, I wanted to cover all my bases, leave no pizza stone unturned. I couldn't stop my mind from racing. We were in week six of *The Great British Baking Contest,* and the competition was getting fierce. I needed to be prepared to defend my weakest spot, my Achilles' heel of baking. And so I kept up the bread-making. Day after boring day.

As much as I despaired, so too did Mildred, my kitchen ghost. Now I was used to Mildred being a bit of a Debbie downer; she was always griping at me for taking the easy way out, using "fancy technology" to whisk or whip or not knowing the "basics," which in her Victorian opinion were plum duff (which didn't, incidentally, have any plums, just suet, dried fruit and egg) or bread made with hop yeast. "Ye begin with hops boiled in water and some potatoes boiled and bruised," she instructed me. Like I didn't have enough recipes to try.

Even Gina, my best friend, refused to come over and do another taste test. "Pops, I don't want to come over and sample rye rusks. Really, love, you're going off the deep end." I felt for her. No doubt she couldn't eat any more combinations of flour, yeast, salt and water plus whatever other ingredients I could dream up. Bread either rises and has good texture and flavor or it doesn't. It's not like cake, where you can hide a multitude of faults under icing.

"Bread is boring," Gina said. "Do your best. You'll be fine."

It was easy for her to brush the crumbs under the carpet and say things would be fine. Gina wasn't a baker; she was a makeup and hair artist—and an excellent one at that. She might think bread was dull, but it was a foundation skill I was going to have to get right. Bread was unforgiving when you messed up, and I couldn't seem to do anything but make a mess.

By the end of the week, I had gone through sacks of flour, fresh yeast, dried yeast, and a sourdough starter I'd made myself weeks ago, and not one single perfect loaf emerged from my frantic efforts. One evening spent in her favorite spot in the kitchen left Gateau, my black cat familiar, looking like she'd been out in a snowstorm. After that, she watched me from an armchair in the living room. Even my own familiar was tired of my klutzy ways.

It wasn't only vanity propelling my desperate attempt at bread mastery. I was worried that if I didn't shine this week, then my days on *The Great British Baking Contest* would be numbered, and then so would my time at Broomewode Hall, *just* when I felt like I was making progress discovering more about my birth parents. I could feel in my gut that my dad was a local, someone from Broomewode Village born and bred, and this week I intended to act on this intuition. Which meant sticking around.

Which is why, by the time Thursday evening was approaching, I'd decided I was going to need some expert help on the bread front. And who better to ask than my coven sister Eve? I called her when I knew she'd be setting up for the dinner shift at the inn. After a nice natter catching up, I explained my predicament and was immediately soothed by Eve's calm manner and her gentle words of encouragement.

"I'm sure it's not that bad, Pops," she said. "You've come so far in the competition. Don't let a bout of nerves throw you off now."

I assured Eve it wasn't nerves. More like a case of breadstick fingers—I couldn't knead dough properly to save my life.

Eve laughed. "Look, if that's really true, then why don't you come to the inn tomorrow morning? On Fridays, Eloise is in the kitchen. She's our pastry chef. She hasn't been here long, but her bread's excellent. I'll have a word with her later and see if she'll give you some tips."

I jumped up and down on the spot, irritating Gateau, who

was napping by my side. I thanked Eve, hung up, and went to face the dreaded mess in my kitchen.

Order your copy today! *Crumbs and Misdemeanors* is Book 6 in the Great Witches Baking Show series.

A Note from Nancy

Dear Reader,

Thank you for reading *The Great Witches Baking Show* series. I am so grateful for all the enthusiasm this series has received. If you enjoyed Poppy's adventures, you're sure to enjoy the *Village Flower Shop,* the *Vampire Knitting Club*, and the *Vampire Book Club* series.

I hope you'll consider leaving a review and please tell your friends who like cozy mysteries and culinary adventures.

Review on Amazon, Goodreads or BookBub. It makes such a difference.

Join my newsletter for a free prequel, *Tangles and Treasons*, the exciting tale of how the gorgeous Rafe Crosyer was turned into a vampire.

I hope to see you in my private Facebook Group. It's a lot of fun. www.facebook.com/groups/NancyWarrenKnitwits

Turn the page for Poppy's recipe for Strawberry and Basil Layer Cake.

Until next time,
Happy Reading,
Nancy

POPPY'S STRAWBERRY AND BASIL
LAYER CAKE

Basil Cream:

As you know, I was short of time for this challenge, so I'd recommend making the basil cream the night before, or at least five hours before you start baking. The four-hour time limit only just didn't cut it for me. I don't want you to have any touch-and-go moments! All in all, you'll probably need to have about five and a half hours to make the whole cake. It's a long time, I know, but it's well worth it. Preparation, preparation, preparation!

Ingredients:

- 6 3/4 cups cold heavy cream
- 60 large basil leaves

Method:

1. Bring 1 1/2 cups cream to a gentle simmer in a

small saucepan over medium heat. And when I say gentle, I mean gentle—we don't want any tears of spilt cream before we even really get started.

2. Bruise large basil leaves by hitting repeatedly with the dull side of a knife (think of your archenemy here and have the same cathartic experience as I did) and then stir the bruised leaves into the cream.

3. Remove from heat, cover tightly with plastic wrap, and let the mixture steep for 25 minutes. Strain through a fine sieve, pressing solids to extract liquid, and then place it into a fridge (or blast chiller if you're short of time and have one nearby!) until the mix is very cold. For most people, this will be at least five hours.

Sponge and Macerated Strawberries

Ingredients:

- 2 sticks unsalted butter, room temperature, plus more for pans
- 3 cups all-purpose flour, plus more for pans
- 2 1/4 teaspoons baking powder
- 1/4 teaspoon baking soda
- Coarse salt
- 1 3/4 cups granulated sugar
- 4 large eggs, room temperature
- 1 1/3 cups low-fat buttermilk, room temperature
- 1 tablespoon pure vanilla extract
- 4 1/2 cups sliced strawberries (1 pound 4 ounces)

- I cup of small (or gently torn) basil leaves
- 3 tablespoons confectioners' sugar

Method

1. Make sure to preheat your oven to 350 degrees, and level your rack so that it sits in center position.
2. Butter two 9-inch round cake pans and then line with parchment cut to fit exactly—we don't want any misshapen sides. Presentation is everything with this cake. Then butter your parchment and dust it with flour, tapping out the excess.
3. Whisk together your flour, baking powder, baking soda, and I teaspoon salt.
4. Beat butter and granulated sugar with a mixer on medium-high speed until pale and fluffy, scraping down sides of bowl as needed, for about 2 minutes. When this is done, reduce your speed to medium, and then add your eggs I at a time, making sure to beat them in well each time.
5. Beat in part of your flour mixture, alternating with buttermilk, but make sure you begin and end with the flour. Then add the vanilla until everything is combined.
6. Divide the batter evenly between pans—be careful here as you want your sponges to come out at exactly the same height.
7. Place them in the oven, wishing them well, of course, and then rotate the tins halfway through, until tops spring back when gently touched and a cake tester inserted into centers comes out clean.

This should take about 40 minutes, but keep on an eye on it, especially for the last five minutes of baking.

8. Transfer your tins to wire racks, and let sponges cool in their tins for 20 minutes.

9. Meanwhile, make the macerated strawberries by combining them with the remaining 1/4 cup sugar, plus more if needed, depending on how sweet your strawberries are already, or how sweet your tooth is! Stir occasionally and leave them for at least 20 minutes and up to an hour if you have the time.

10. Once the cakes are cooled, run a knife around their edges, turn them out onto separate plates and make sure they have time to cool down completely.

11. While the cakes are cooling, get your basil cream infusion, and using a mixer, whisk the basil cream with the confectioners' sugar in the chilled bowl on a high speed until soft peaks form.

12. Very, very gently add the macerated strawberries, making sure you keep back a handful of berries and all of the juices to drizzle over the top of the cake. Add a few more small (or torn) basil leaves to the cream.

13. Now layer each sponge cake with the basil mix.

14. Use the remainder of the basil cream to spoon over the top of the cake and pile the macerated strawberries on top.

Bon appétit!

∾

Village Flower Shop: Paranormal Cozy Mystery

Peony Dreadful - Book 1

Karma Camellia - Book 2

Highway to Hellebore - Book 3

Vampire Knitting Club: Paranormal Cozy Mystery

Tangles and Treasons - a free prequel for Nancy's newsletter subscribers

The Vampire Knitting Club - Book 1

Stitches and Witches - Book 2

Crochet and Cauldrons - Book 3

Stockings and Spells - Book 4

Purls and Potions - Book 5

Fair Isle and Fortunes - Book 6

Lace and Lies - Book 7

Bobbles and Broomsticks - Book 8

Popcorn and Poltergeists - Book 9

Garters and Gargoyles - Book 10

Diamonds and Daggers - Book 11

Herringbones and Hexes - Book 12

Ribbing and Runes - Book 13

Mosaics and Magic - Book 14

Cat's Paws and Curses - A Holiday Whodunnit

Vampire Knitting Club Boxed Set: Books 1-3

Vampire Knitting Club Boxed Set: Books 4-6

Vampire Knitting Club Boxed Set: Books 7-9

Vampire Knitting Club Boxed Set: Books 10-12

Vampire Book Club: A Paranormal Women's Fiction Cozy Mystery

Crossing the Lines - Prequel

The Vampire Book Club - Book 1

Chapter and Curse - Book 2

A Spelling Mistake - Book 3

A Poisonous Review - Book 4

Abigail Dixon: A 1920s Cozy Historical Mystery

In 1920s Paris everything is très chic, except murder.

Death of a Flapper - Book 1

Toni Diamond Mysteries

Toni is a successful saleswoman for Lady Bianca Cosmetics in this series of humorous cozy mysteries.

Frosted Shadow - Book 1

Ultimate Concealer - Book 2

Midnight Shimmer - Book 3

A Diamond Choker For Christmas - A Holiday Whodunnit

Toni Diamond Mysteries Boxed Set: Books 1-4

The Almost Wives Club: Contemporary Romantic Comedy

An enchanted wedding dress is a matchmaker in this series of romantic comedies where five runaway brides find out who the best men really are!

The Almost Wives Club: Kate - Book 1

Secondhand Bride - Book 2

Bridesmaid for Hire - Book 3

The Wedding Flight - Book 4

If the Dress Fits - Book 5

The Almost Wives Club Boxed Set: Books 1-5

Take a Chance: Contemporary Romance

Meet the Chance family, a cobbled together family of eleven kids who are all grown up and finding their ways in life and love.

Chance Encounter - Prequel

Kiss a Girl in the Rain - Book 1

Iris in Bloom - Book 2

Blueprint for a Kiss - Book 3

Every Rose - Book 4

Love to Go - Book 5

The Sheriff's Sweet Surrender - Book 6

The Daisy Game - Book 7

Take a Chance Boxed Set: Prequel and Books 1-3

For a complete list of books, check out Nancy's website at NancyWarrenAuthor.com

ABOUT THE AUTHOR

Nancy Warren is the USA Today Bestselling author of more than 100 novels. She's originally from Vancouver, Canada, though she tends to wander and has lived in England, Italy and California at various times. While living in Oxford she dreamed up The Vampire Knitting Club. Favorite moments include being the answer to a crossword puzzle clue in Canada's National Post newspaper, being featured on the front page of the New York Times when her book Speed Dating launched Harlequin's NASCAR series, and being nominated three times for Romance Writers of America's RITA award. She has an MA in Creative Writing from Bath Spa University. She's an avid hiker, loves chocolate and most of all, loves to hear from readers!

The best way to stay in touch is to sign up for Nancy's newsletter at NancyWarrenAuthor.com or www.facebook.com/groups/NancyWarrenKnitwits

To learn more about Nancy and her books
NancyWarrenAuthor.com

facebook.com/AuthorNancyWarren

twitter.com/nancywarren1

instagram.com/nancywarrenauthor

amazon.com/Nancy-Warren/e/B001H6NM5Q

goodreads.com/nancywarren

bookbub.com/authors/nancy-warren

Made in the USA
Middletown, DE
09 July 2023

34772420R00126